Nathan Goodman

Protocol One

THOUGHT REACH PRESS, a publishing division of Thought Reach, LLC. United States of America.

ISBN: 978-1542478274

First Thought Reach Press printing March, 2017

For information regarding special discounts for bulk purchases, or permission to reproduce any content other than mentioned above, contact the publisher at support@thoughtreach.com.

Printed in the USA, the United Kingdom, and Canada except where otherwise stated.

The Special Agent Jana Baker Spy-Thriller Series, by Nathan **Goodman**

Protocol One

The Fourteenth Protocol

Protocol 15

Breach of Protocol

Get a free copy of book 2 in this series, *The Fourteenth Protocol.* See details inside.

To those people that serve in our military, federal agencies, police forces and others. You sacrifice so that freedom lives on, and we will never forget you for it.

1

A Communique Intercepted

Headquarters, Federal Bureau of Investigation, J. Edgar Hoover Building, 935 Pennsylvania Avenue NW, Washington, DC. "Is this the intercepted communiqué that NSA sent over?"

"Yes, sir," the junior FBI agent said as he held up a printout.

FBI Supervisory Special Agent Steven Bolz read the document. "What makes them think this communication is any more important than the thousands of others they're intercepting? Al-Qaeda has been sending messages like these for the last nine months."

The junior agent pulled against the neckline of his starched white-collar shirt and shifted in his seat.

Bolz looked at him. "Who sent this over?"

"Came in on the secure line, sir. The NSA analyst said it had gone through channels, and that it was level ten."

"Level ten? All this communiqué indicates is a series of coordinates. And you said these coordinates correspond to places spread out across the Middle East? That's not a level ten, that doesn't even rate a level five in my book. Get him on the line."

"Yes, sir."

Bolz took the receiver and waited for an answer. After the third ring, what sounded like a teenager's voice answered, "NSA operation center, this is Knuckles."

"Did you say your name was Knuckles?" Agent Bolz said as he placed one hand on his hip.

"Oh, Agent Bolz, you must be calling about that level ten. How can I help, sir?"

"How old are you? Oh, never mind. Did you do the analysis on this communication?"

"No, sir, one of my people did. I'm the senior supervisory duty analyst, sir. My duties are to ensure the veracity of claims made by analysts on my team."

"You're in a supervisory role? You can't be more than fifteen years old. How did you get this job? Look, son, we don't have time to track down every communication made by a terror network. There are too many, you've got to narrow it down more than that."

Sitting in the vast NSA command center at Fort Meade, Maryland, Knuckles rubbed his chin, a chin that could barely produce peach fuzz. Those around him would say he looked fourteen years old, maybe fifteen on a good day. But those same people had come to respect him the way a student respects a professor.

"Agent Bolz, I've personally analyzed over eleven thousand intercepts from terror cells all over the world. I am the senior-most member of the terror watch group. I *train* NSA analysts and personnel from all over the intelligence community. And that includes the intelligence services of our allies. My age is not in question here, sir. Not to mention the fact that my section chief, Bill Tarleton, reviewed the communiqué before we sent it to you. If you are second-guessing the importance of this communication, I'd suggest you take a closer look at the identity of the US citizen in question, then call me back." The line went dead.

Agent Bolz's mouth hung open and he stared at the receiver. "Well that little son of a bitch. Call him back? I've been at the bureau longer than he's been alive. Who does he think he is?" Bolz turned to the junior agent. "All right, run the identity of the US citizen in question. Check it against the terror watch list, see if he's in the NCIC database, then check him against Interpol."

"Already done, sir," the junior agent said as he handed another piece of paper to Agent Bolz. The young man's hand shook, yet Bolz did not notice.

"Well why didn't you say so?" Bolz studied the paper. "Well I'll be damned." His eyes traced further and further down the sheet. "The chief financial officer of Petrolsoft? Good God. That's a multibillion-dollar corporation. No wonder NSA put priority on this. We never get an intercept with people of this type communicating to anyone on the terror watch list."

"Sir?" The young agent said. "What does Petrolsoft do?"

"Giant software conglomerate, Wall Street darling. Then a few years back they purchased several manufacturers of oil-well-drilling equipment and other equipment needed in oil production facilities. I own some shares myself." Bolz rubbed his temple, lost in thought. Then, just under his breath he said, "Now why is the CFO of a multibillion-dollar oil conglomerate conversing with Al-Qaeda?"

2

The Interview

Headquarters of Petrolsoft Corporation, Midtown Manhattan, 160 Madison Avenue, New York.

Jana Baker sat in front of the mahogany desk and hoped the interview would end soon. It was going well but her nerves were getting the best of her. She quietly congratulated herself for getting this far. The man sitting behind the desk was none other than billionaire Rune Dima, Petrolsoft's founder and chief executive officer. Jana focused all her effort to maintain eye contact and avoid glancing out the glass wall behind him into the stunning view of Manhattan's skyline.

"Well, Miss Baker, your credentials are outstanding. BBA from Georgetown University, very impressive. Number two in your class, very impressive indeed. I see you've passed your Series 6 and Series 7 exams in record time. Sounds like you'd like to be a Wall Street trader one day? Working the floor of the stock exchange, perhaps? And your resume also says you were captain of the track team. How did you have time to be captain of the track team and maintain that GPA? Now, you realize that you are interviewing for an intern position? It seems way below your skill level, if you don't mind my saying. Anyone with the aptitude to pass the Series 7, General Securities Representative Exam at your age has particular ambitions."

Jana readjusted her hands; it was as if she did not know where to put them.

"Yes, sir. My goal is to be involved in international stock trading and investing one day. This might be just an intern position, but working directly for the CEO, executing stock trades at your direction, would be invaluable experience."

"I usually prefer my interns to still be at university."

"And why is that, if I might ask?" she said.

"They are less likely to leave after a few months. But you, you could get any number of different jobs."

"Sir, I know you feel like you're taking a risk with me, but I'll make you a promise. You bring me on as your intern, and I'll stay in that role for a minimum twelve months."

"A twelve-month commitment before an employee finds a better opportunity is hardly worth my time, Miss Baker."

Jana smiled. "You'll have promoted me by then, sir."

He stood and extended a hand.

"Congratulations, Miss Baker. You start tomorrow morning. We can use the help. We've got some investing of our own to do. But the global oil technology business is unforgiving. We work long days here, so be prepared."

"Thank you, sir. You won't regret your decision."

He grinned. "I'd better not."

Jana walked out of the office and struggled to restrain the grin that was beginning to form on her face, not wanting the other office workers to think she was cocky. She pulled the door closed behind her, readjusted the tight pony tail restraining her silky blonde hair, and tugged her suit jacket. This might be just an intern position, but it was the beginning of what she had planned, a career in the lucrative field of international trading and investments.

After she had left, a lean man with slick black hair and dark olive-colored skin walked into the office of the CEO, Rune Dima, and let the door close behind him. His clothes screamed young New York wealth.

"Did you see the ass on that thing?" the man said.

"Jeffrey." It was mild rebuke.

"Oh come on. Now tell me you wouldn't like to tap that."

"The interns in this office are not yours to have sex with, Jeffrey. Granted, she is a beautiful young woman. But if you want to succeed as an executive, where your subordinates are concerned, you will have to keep your fly zipped. You are the chief financial officer of one of the top technology companies in the world. Remember, we are not in our homeland. Here, bad things happen to the stock valuations of companies like ours if a scandal hits Wall Street, particularly in this country. And with what we have planned, we have no room for scandal. The only way our plan works is if our stock valuation stays at current levels."

"You hired her, didn't you?" Jeffrey smiled.

"Yes."

"I knew it," he said as he clapped his hands together and laughed. "And don't hand me that politically correct crap. Let me guess, she was the most beautiful female applicant for the position? A trim body, long blonde hair down to the center of her back, legs up to here, and a nice tight—"

"Enough. I won't tolerate this kind of behavior, from you or anyone. She's off limits, is that understood? And besides, what makes you think she has a such a great figure? That double-breasted business suit she was wearing obscures anything you might think you are seeing."

"Oh, the hot body is there. Believe me, it's there. Come on,

Rune, don't be such a hard-ass. Tell me her name."

"You haven't heard a word I've said, have you? Jana Baker. She has an BBA with a major in finance from Georgetown, Jeffrey. Graduated second in her class. She's not a play toy. Already passed her Series 7 exam. And based on the project she ran during her prior internship at our competitor, Oracle, she'll be invaluable."

"And all with a body like that."

"You never quit, do you?"

"I'm afraid not, cousin. Not until I get what I want, that is."

3

Dean and Deluca

Two weeks later, Midtown Manhattan.

With the sunlight just cresting the buildings, Jana walked south on Fifth Avenue past Rockefeller Plaza and turned down Forty-Eighth. It was quicker to come this way in order to go into Dean and Deluca to grab a cup of coffee. Her budget didn't allow her to make a regular habit of buying specialty foods from the retailer, but the place smelled like a little slice of heaven, and Jana couldn't resist. The line at the coffee bar was short, unusual for this time of morning; a sign Jana was starting Monday off right.

"Help you?" the man behind the coffee bar said to her.

"A medium Manhattan blend, please."

"Yes, ma'am. That will be five eighteen with tax. How would you like to pay for that?"

A man standing just to her side reached across and put his hand on Jana's shoulder. His physical contact wasn't overtly sexual, in fact, to an onlooker, it would have looked more like the way a father puts his arm around a daughter.

"I'll get that," he said as he handed a credit card to the barista. "Make it two." He withdrew the hand from her shoulder as quickly as he had placed it there.

"Excuse me," Jana said as she shifted away and looked at the man. He was wearing a crisp navy business suit and looked to be in his early fifties. Her look of disapproval was obvious, and to Jana, it was apparent he was hitting on her. "That *won't* be necessary."

"Oh it's no problem." He leaned closer, but his eyes scanned over the tops of shelves and across the store; it was as if he was looking for someone. He then leveled a gaze at her. "How's the internship going?"

"What? Oh, you must work at Petrolsoft too. Sorry, I don't recognize you. Did we meet already?"

He ignored the question. "As the assistant to the CEO, you must have fairly unrestricted access across the corporate intranet. Am I right?"

"Excuse me?"

He crossed his arms. "Don't you find it interesting the amount of investing going on over there?"

"Look, I don't know who you think you are but—" She stopped as the barista pushed two coffees across the counter.

"Cream and sugar are over there," he said while pointing.

The man continued. "Investing in oil futures, that is."

Jana paused. "I can't talk about things that go on at Petrolsoft. Do you work there or not?"

"What's concerning is that Petrolsoft seems to be making an awfully large bet that the oil market is about to skyrocket. A dangerous bet, in fact."

"I don't know anything about—"

He smiled. "Of course you do, Miss Baker. You're the assistant to the CEO. You see everything that comes across his desk, and you're the one making the buys."

Jana began a swift walk toward the exit, but stopped and turned. "How do you know my name?"

He quoted from memory, "Jana Michelle Baker. Born October 19, 1986. The only daughter of Richard and Lillian Baker. Father, died 10/29/1988. Mother, deceased also, died November 8, 1993. You graduated summa cum laude from Georgetown University with a bachelor of business administration, and you just passed the Series 7 stock broker's exam."

Her eyes flared. "What the hell is this? Are you stalking me? You want me to call a cop?"

The man simply smiled. "We'll be in touch." He walked past her and said, "Oh, you might not want to mention our conversation to anyone, especially anyone at Petrolsoft."

As Jana's mouth hung open, he exited through glass double doors and disappeared into brilliant morning sunlight pouring into the front of the store. He was gone.

4

Comraderie

The man walked up West Forty-Eighth Street and took the first right onto Rockefeller Plaza, a street normally blocked to all nonofficial traffic. He slid open the door of a white van parked there and got in.

"You get the tracker in place?" a man in the back of the van said to him.

"Larry, Larry, Larry. Of course I got it in place."

"Well don't be like that with me," Larry replied. "I wasn't the one to bounce you out of bed at four this morning."

"No, you're not. Sorry, didn't mean to snap at you."

"Sounds like somebody's regretting not retiring? Come on, Chuck, you hit twenty years of service over three years ago. How come you decided to keep working? Don't you have a beach to retire to or something?"

"A beach? As if a guy on a federal pension can afford a place on the beach."

"Well still, after twenty-three years with the FBI, you should take a break. You've got some savings. Go live it up a little. You don't need to still be slogging around the streets of Manhattan, working cases."

"But I enjoy the commute from Trenton so much."

The van pulled into Forty-Eighth Avenue traffic and drove away.

"You enjoy the commute from Trenton? Trenton is, what, a two-hour slog through humanity? Each way, I might add?"

"Well, nobody told me I'd get rich at the bureau. Trenton is the closest thing to Manhattan I can afford."

"Damn, Stone. The divorce really took it out of you, didn't it?"

Agent Chuck Stone had worked a myriad of cases in his time as a special agent with the FBI, and this one had started no differently than most of the others. What was different this time was Chuck's reassignment to the FBI's New York field office.

The Jacob Javit's Federal Building at 26 Federal Plaza sat nestled into the Civic Center district in Lower Manhattan. The building, first opened in 1969, housed several federal agencies. But it was the FBI that took occupancy of the entire twenty-third floor. From this vantage point, agents on duty the morning of September 11, 2001 had been witness to the terror attacks on the World Trade Centers, which once stood a distance just nine football fields away. Most agents had no choice but to stand helplessly and watch as the buildings collapsed.

"Well," Stone said, "divorce ain't cheap. Hey, did I ever tell you that when she moved out, she even took the ice trays out of the freezer?"

"Took the ice trays out of the freezer? You mean to tell me you came home from work, found she had moved her stuff out, *and* she had taken the plastic ice trays with her? What a psycho."

"Tell me about it. Hey, check the tracking device. I stuck it to the subject's shoulder, but those damn things are so finicky. Make sure it's working."

"Yeah, yeah. I've got it right here," Agent Larry Fry said, pointing to the laptop monitor. On the screen, a blip pulsed on the map of Manhattan's midtown district. "Looks like she grabbed a cab or something. She's headed down Fifth right now, toward the headquarters of Petrolsoft."

"Don't you just love the start of a new case?" Stone said.

"Love the start of a case? As opposed to the end, when we kick down a door and arrest a terrorist or other such asshole?"

"Yeah, I mean, think about it. I've been doing this for twenty-three years, and I tell you, the start of a case still gets to me. It's like the beginning of a relationship with a woman, you know? Everything is new, so much to discover."

"You mean the sex is great at the beginning of a relationship."

Agent Stone looked at him. "No, that's not what I mean. Not that what you said isn't true. But no, I'm talking about the energy, the excitement."

"Yeah, the sex. I know."

Stone laughed. "How old are you, Fry? Twenty-nine? Thirty?"

"Twenty-nine. Why?"

"You young guys. Wait till you get to be my age. Now don't get me wrong. A fifty-one-year-old thinks about sex, but . . . how do I put this? At this age, we find it easier to concentrate on the case we're working instead of on our balls."

It was Fry's turn to laugh. "You are the simplest SOB I've ever met."

"Well, laugh it up. I still like the beginning of a case. You never know where it might lead."

As the van driver turned south on Fifth Avenue to follow the blip on the map—a beacon signal emanating from the tiny tracking device Agent Stone had placed on Jana Baker's business jacket—Agent Fry said, "That reminds me. Since I was just assigned this surveillance an hour ago, I haven't even seen a picture of the target. What's she look like?"

Stone ran his hand across the front of his scalp where fewer hairs remained than in his younger days. He said, "You just want to know if she's hot."

"Well?"

"Man, eight million residents in the city, and what? At least half of them have to be female. And you have your sights set on the one woman we're supposed to recruit to work as an undercover informant?"

"You going to tell me?"

Stone exhaled. "Yes, she's attractive. You happy now?"

"Ah, come on, Agent Stone. You're thinking the same thing as me."

"Fry, she's less than half my age. She's a twenty-two-year-old, just out of college. I'm more than old enough to be her father. So no, I'm not thinking the same as you."

"You know I'm just messing with you, right?" Fry said.

"Just so you know, if you want a career here, you can't get attracted to anyone in the scope of the investigation. It clouds your judgment, distracts you."

Fry shook his head. "They were right."

"Who was right?" Stone said.

"They told me this was how you were. They said you'd picked up the nickname of 'Pops' by the other agents. Said you're always fathering the younger guys."

"Pops, huh? Yeah, I've heard that one myself. So let that be a lesson to you, sonny. You young whippersnappers need to listen to the advice of us old-timers."

"So what's your advice to me on this case?"

"Keep your hands off of our material witness."

5

Cautious Exhilaration

Jana's mouth hung open as the man disappeared out the door. "What in the hell was that about?" she said as questions swirled in her mind. *Who is that guy? And how does he know so much about me? And I'm not supposed to mention this conversation to anyone? How could I not?*

The man knew specific details about Jana and her background. *Who knows things like that? And who approaches someone then randomly spouts off their life history? Someone who has been looking into your background,* Jana thought.

Still, as she exited the door of Dean and Deluca and flagged down a cab, she couldn't help but notice a tinge of excitement building inside. *And he said not to mention it to anyone at Petrolsoft specifically.*

Several minutes later, her cab pulled up to Petrolsoft's main entrance just as a text message buzzed on her phone. The incoming number was listed as *Blocked.* Jana got out of the car and began weaving in and out of people on the sidewalk, but when she read the message, her mouth again fell open.

Hope you enjoy your coffee.
Lunch—12:30—Shanghai Mung Bistro,
W. 32nd St., An Asian place about

1.5 blocks from your office.
It's crowded, but you'll find me.
Come alone.

"Who *is* this guy?" she said as she came to an abrupt stop. A man walking down the sidewalk sidestepped her and glared. She was talking to herself and she knew it. "What are you looking at?"

Jana walked through the massive set of black glass double doors, the entrance to Petrolsoft's corporate headquarters, and shouldered her way into an overcrowded elevator. Jammed in the throngs of humanity on their way to work in one of the world's most lucrative software companies, Jana felt small.

Her common sense told her to stay away from the stranger. But there was something about him, something in the look of his eyes that she couldn't quite place. The eyes were soft, disarming; the kind of eyes you'd see when you looked at your father. Based on what he'd said, the details he knew about her, she *should* be afraid. But she wasn't; she had a feeling of exhilaration. And she had to admit, her curiosity had been piqued.

She knew she'd walk to the next block at lunchtime to come face-to-face with the man. Besides, he was right. *A public place.* Every restaurant on West Thirty-Second would be packed at that hour. *What could go wrong?*

Being new to Manhattan had its disadvantages though. For one thing, Jana knew virtually no one. She'd only been here three weeks and her microscopic studio apartment still had boxes stacked against one wall. The exhilaration she felt upon meeting the stranger was one thing, but in the crush of people in the elevator, she felt very alone. The feeling was familiar to her.

When Jana was just two years old, her father had passed away. She had no recollection of being told that he was gone, but what

16

she did have was tiny fragments of memories of him. A little flash here, a flicker of a face there. To Jana, thinking about her father was like watching an old newsreel whose image quality was so low, only fragments survived. There was one memory though, that stuck in her mind. It must have been not long before he died and Jana was standing on the living room couch, looking out the large bay windows onto the front lawn of their North Carolina home. These were the only solid images of her father she could muster.

He was outside, snow up over his ankles, and he bent down to form a snowball. Two-year-old Jana giggled endlessly as he threw snowballs at the window. She laughed so hard she flopped onto the couch over and over, only to stand back up again.

As the elevator doors opened for the fourth time on its way to the sixty-third and uppermost floor, several people exited and one man got on. For just a moment she thought she smelled her father's aftershave.

6

Office of the CEO

Petrolsoft Headquarters. Office of the CEO.

"Sit down, Jeffrey. We need to talk about the plan. How far along are you?"

"Relax, cousin. Everything is on schedule. We've been diversifying our banking and investments over the last six months in order to keep a low profile. Don't want to attract the attention of the Securities and Exchange Commission, if you know what I mean. But I need help. Transferring this much money between so many banks is getting to be a problem. I don't have that kind of time."

"We'll work on that. But the SEC is the least of our worries. We just need to stay below the radar of the NSA and their damn eavesdropping. Continue."

"I've been very careful. We have relocated the bulk of our liquid assets to banks in Milan, Rome, London, Geneva, and the Cayman Islands."

"And what did the analysts at Goldman Sachs have to say about that on the last quarterly conference call?"

"Nothing really. He just wanted to know why. I told him we have always had an interest in diversification. You know, spread your assets across the global banking system—a bet that insulates us from a recession in the US."

Rune smiled. "And they bought that crap?"

"Well, sure. Have I ever let you down?"

"And how about the other half of the plan? Has the virus been embedded into our next software release?"

"Of course. I told you, I'm on top of it. The virus is planted in the next build. Helix version 6.7.8001 just finished quality assurance testing. It goes out to our controlled release customers first. Two weeks later, we deploy it to our software-as-a-service cloud hosting environments, and that's when it will filter down to the rest of our customers. The virus will infect their systems and we'll then be ready to execute."

Rune leaned across his desk toward his cousin, Jeffrey Dima, and said, "And you're sure the virus code is not going to be detected by our own software development staff?"

"Positive. It's highly obfuscated. Not even the development engineers have any idea it's there."

"I'll grant you this. You are good, Jeffrey. You are good."

"I know," he said through a laugh. "Hey, how's that intern? You bagged her yet?"

"I told you to leave it alone. We are too far into the plan to get distracted by a pretty face."

"Oh come on, we're ahead of schedule. By the time we execute this thing, the international trading markets won't even know what happened. And you and I will be rich beyond our imaginations." Jeffrey turned and began to grin, then yelled over his shoulder. "Miss Baker? Can you come in here a minute?"

"Yes, sir," came Jana's reply from her desk outside the CEO's office.

"What the hell are you doing?" Rune said as he scowled at Jeffrey.

"Oh, relax."

"Yes, sir?" Jana said as she walked through the door and up to Rune's desk.

Rune looked flustered but was quick to think on his feet. "Have you finished the research on all the hedge funds we discussed?"

"Almost done now, sir. But are you sure the only ones you needed financials on were those with the bulk of their investments in the oil and gas industry? You don't want to look at others with more diversified portfolios?"

Jeffrey stared at Jana from behind and his eyes traced down the back of her body.

"Yes, Miss Baker," Rune said. "That will be all. Thank you."

"And you want me to open accounts at all of the hedge funds, sir? You don't want to review the list first?"

"No, I don't need to review it. I've seen over the past weeks just how thorough your work is. Just open the accounts and when Jeffrey asks, you can get the information to him."

"Yes, sir." Jana was out the door but turned around and leaned back into the office. She couldn't help but notice Jeffrey's eyes had followed her and were now locked onto her chest. When he finally made eye contact, he turned his attention to the laptop in his hands, where he slid his right forefinger across a small fingerprint scanner. As his identity was verified, the laptop monitor blinked to life.

What a slimeball, she thought.

"Oh, sir," Jana said. "I'm about to head down for lunch."

"That's fine," Rune replied. "Just close the door behind you."

After Jana was gone, Jeffrey smiled. "Hey Rune, what color do you think her panties are?"

This time, Rune stood and his fists formed on the surface of the mahogany desk. "For the last time, drop it. I'm not going to tell you again."

"You've changed, cousin. When we were kids in our homeland, you were nothing like this."

"Yes, I *was* like this. You were just too busy trying to separate virgins from the clothing they were wearing to notice. This company is my world now. I have loyalty to our homeland and our cause, certainly, but don't cross me on this."

Jeffrey stood to leave. "You have lost touch with the old ways, and it's made you soft. You may be CEO of this company, but I am the one in contact with our friends in Aleppo."

Rune launched from his chair as a vein on his temple pulsed. He pushed Jeffrey against the wall. "Soft? Soft you say? What the hell do you think we're doing here? We're about to pull off what will be looked at in future years as the start of *everything*. We're about to crush the national economy of the United States. Our people, the funding we're going to have our hands on? We'll be able to finance any attack we want. This is an attack against the beast, and I intend to inflict as much damage as possible."

Jeffrey pushed him back. "The damage we're about to inflict? What a load of crap. This is not the way of the jihadist. This is the way of the coward. The jihadist takes human life, and as much of it as possible."

"You don't like our plan? And I suppose you would say that to the face of Abu Adim Al-Jawary? And where did you think we were going to obtain funding to pay for all those bigger, full-scale attacks he and bin Laden have planned? Huh? Where did you think they were going to get the funds to purchase a nuclear weapon in the first place? It takes money, Jeffrey, lots of money." He turned and walked to his desk. "And I, for one, intend to do what I set out to do. You can either get with the program, or . . ." Rune trailed off.

"Or what? Don't threaten me, cousin. I'm in this too deeply. And I'm the only one Al-Jawary will communicate with, not you. You need me and you know it."

7

To Convince a Witness

Shanghai Mung Asian Bistro, W. Thirty-Second Street, New York. About one and a half blocks from Petrolsoft HQ.

Jana rung her hands for the third time on the short elevator ride down to the lobby. *What in the hell am I doing?* She thought to herself. *I mean, this guy could be a psycho. But no,* she rationalized, *psychos don't walk up to you like that. This is something else, something bigger.* She was beginning to talk to herself on the short walk. "I'm going to peek my head in there and see if I spot him. Then I'll decide."

To Jana the walk to the restaurant felt like it took forever. As one foot stepped in front of the other, she felt like the sidewalk was moving backwards, as if she was moving in slow motion. Her nerves were getting the better of her.

The street was bustling. By this time of day all the delivery trucks had cleared, but cars jammed the one-way street and a few honked their horns. The sidewalk was clogged with humanity moving in both directions and Jana felt claustrophobic.

When she got to the restaurant, she peered into the large front window, but the reflection was so strong the only thing she could see was herself. The front door burst open and four Chinese businessmen walked out, the aroma of fresh-sautéed Kung Pau chicken followed them. She leaned into the door and scanned the crowded tables. Most were full and several people stood to the side, waiting to be seated. But as the door swung closed, it almost hit her in the head.

Oh, this is crazy, she thought as the grip on her purse tightened. *What was I thinking?* But no sooner had she turned to walk away did the man lean his way through the door. He had shed his business jacket and his tie was loosened. He raised a white paper napkin to wipe the glistening perspiration off his forehead and said, "You've got to try the Kung Pau. Spicy as hell."

She clutched her purse tighter but was again disarmed by the familiar look of sedate calmness in his eyes.

Jana hesitated.

"Really, it's a full restaurant," he said with a smile. "You're perfectly safe. Come on." He pushed the door open wider.

She followed him inside, shuffling sideways through the tight rows of tables. It wasn't until he went to sit down that Jana noticed a holstered firearm tucked against the back of his right hip. "Have a seat," he motioned. "Are you up for the challenge?"

For the first time, Jana spoke. "What challenge?"

"The Kung Pau. It's a killer."

Jana glanced at his half-eaten plate of food.

A woman dressed in traditional Chinese waitress attire leaned in. "Are you ready, ma'am? What can I get you?" she said with a pad and pen in hand.

"Ah, I'll have the Kung Pau, and a glass of sweet tea, please."

"Ma'am?"

The man smiled as he stabbed another piece of chicken with his fork. "I don't think the sweetened brewed tea you grew up with on your grandfather's farm is something the New York crowd knows much about."

"Hot tea is fine," Jana said to the waitress, who disappeared toward the kitchen as quickly as she had arrived. "Who are you, and why do you know so much about me?"

"Sorry for all the secrecy." He held out his hand. "Special Agent Chuck Stone, FBI."

"FBI? What does the FBI want with me?" Jana thought further. "Can I see your credentials, please?"

He held out an aged leather wallet that enclosed his badge and identification. "You said something about not mentioning our meeting with my employer."

"Let me get right to the point, Miss Baker. We've done a thorough background check on you. Sorry. We do that kind of thing before we approach someone."

Again, thought Jana, *it's the eyes. And something about when he smiles. The way the skin crinkles around the eyes. He reminds me of . . .*

"And why did you do that?" she said as she grabbed his wrist, the act blocking his fork's path to his mouth.

"Sorry, I didn't catch breakfast. We run backgrounds on people before we approach them to ask for their help in a case."

"What kind of case?"

"Miss Baker, before I go any further, you have to understand, I brought you here because it would be nearly impossible for us to be eavesdropped on. This place is packed with the local Asian community. This conversation, the one you and I are having? It can never make it back to your employer."

"Why not?"

He scanned the other diners and spoke just loud enough to be heard over the bustling conversations. "Because it would be a felony for you to act in a manner that would jeopardize a federal investigation."

"You're investigating Petrolsoft? My employer isn't a criminal organization, Agent Stone. What is it you think they have done?"

"Well, nothing yet. But it's who your boss is talking to that has us concerned."

"Mr. Dima?" Jana said as she crossed her arms. "You're investigating Rune Dima? He's as gentle as a kitten." Jana's forehead furled.

"Not Rune Dima, Jeffrey Dima, the CFO."

"I'm the assistant to the chief executive officer, but yes, I suppose you could say I also work for the CFO. But let's stop right there. Is it a crime in this country to talk to someone? Who is he talking to?"

Agent Stone's eyes became cold. "Abu Adim Al-Jawary, a Syrian national."

Jana began to feel heat rise around her collar and she shifted in her seat.

"And who is that?"

"Al-Jawary is the number three in Al-Qaeda, Miss Baker. That's right, Al-Qaeda, the terror organization founded by none other than Osama bin Laden himself, a name I'm sure you are familiar with."

She leaned toward him. "Let me see if I get this right. You think Jeffrey Dima is talking to terrorists? Are you out of your mind?"

"It's not that I *think* he's talking to terrorists, Miss Baker. A communiqué from Al-Jawary was intercepted by the National Security Agency. It originated in Aleppo, Syria, from an encrypted cell phone believed used by Al-Jawary, and was sent to none other than your CFO, Jeffrey Dima."

"I don't believe you," Jana said as she squirmed in her seat.

The waitress returned and placed a plate of sizzling food in front of her. "Can I get you anything else?"

"No, thank you," Stone said while maintaining eye contact with Jana. The waitress departed. "Miss Baker, I've been doing this for twenty-three years. I know what I'm doing." His eyes drifted toward the front door, where more patrons exited. He then looked Jana in the eye. "You believe me. You just don't want to believe me." He took a bite of food. "If I'm in your shoes, I'm thinking the same thing. You've scored the perfect internship. The things you'll learn about international business working at the side of one of the most successful CEOs in North America. It's got to have its allure. But make no mistake, Miss Baker, this is real and it's happening right underneath your nose."

Jana fought the flush forming on her face and neck. "Why me? Why are you telling me all this?"

"Because we need your help. We need someone on the inside."

"You want me to spy on my boss?"

"Yes."

"Well I won't do it. I already told you, Rune Dima is as gentle as a kitten. And Jeffrey, well Jeffrey is a bit of a prick, but he hardly seems the type. He wouldn't be involved in anything like this."

She stood to leave but Stone placed a gentle hand on her wrist and held it.

"You stay, I'll go. This has all got to be overwhelming for you, but you believe it." He stood and wiped his mouth, then dropped two twenty-dollar bills on the table. As Jana sat back down, he leaned his hands onto the table. "Jana, we're going to take Jeffrey Dima down, and when we do, we're taking others with him. We always do. You can either be part of the solution, or get swept up in the investigation. It's your choice." He threw his business jacket on. "Eat something. You look pale, it will be good for you. I'll be in touch." Before he left, he said one last thing. "Jana, remember, I'm one of the good guys."

Jana's eyes followed him as he disappeared out the door.

She shook her head and looked at the steam rising from her plate. "Three weeks on the internship of a lifetime, and I end up working in a pit of vipers. Nice going, Jana. Welcome to New York."

The encounter left her asking as many questions as had just been answered. But what overpowered her was a new-felt fear, the fear that Agent Stone was right. He *was* one of the good guys. How she knew that she wasn't sure, but she kept thinking about his eyes. There was something so familiar, so *safe*, about them. Looking into them reminded her of growing up. It was a feeling she couldn't shake. He was disarming and somehow Jana felt comfortable with him.

Her mind drifted back to childhood, a time when things were so clear and simple. It had all gone bad one terrible day in second grade. She remembered it with vivid clarity. She had been sitting in class when the school nurse had come and whispered something to the teacher, Miss Hancock. "Jana?" the teacher said, her voice soft like silk sheets. "Can you take your book bag and get your coat? Miss Peterson will walk with you." Jana had no idea why she would need to leave class, much less leave the school, but complied without hesitation. The school nurse took her hand and walked to the principal's office. Jana's stomach quelled into nervous rumbling. There, through the glass, Jana could see a uniformed sheriff's deputy. She had no idea what was about to happen, but the feeling she was in some kind of trouble was overwhelming, and her hands began to shake. The deputy knelt down on one knee and said something she never forgot. "There's been a terrible accident, a car accident. Miss Baker, I'm sorry to have to tell you this, but your mother has been killed."

Jana heard nothing after that, although her memory recorded the vision of mouths moving.

Jana's world came crashing down that bleak winter morning, and now as an adult, she wasn't sure she had ever recovered.

8

Avon Street

Avon Street Apartments, Queens, New York.

That evening, a rap at the door of Jana's aging studio apartment caused her to startle. The Queens walk-up was tiny, microscopic even, yet clean. Jana had felt lucky to find a place she could live without a roommate. After college, she had grown tired of the inevitable clashes in personality with one roommate or another. The girls she had lived with were great, but each had her own quirks. The first had been a night owl, an innocent enough behavior, but something that kept Jana up till all hours of the night. The next was a sweetheart as well, but made too much a habit of showing up with new bunkmates, guys that Jana would find staring at her when she woke up in the morning. Then finally, there was Alene. Alene had been the best of all, but Jana had never been able to convince her the habit of constantly burning incense was giving her headaches. To Alene, the soft aroma was soothing. In Jana's opinion, it was just a leftover practice from the hippie days of the 1970s.

Jana walked to the door and looked through the peephole. The receding hairline of Agent Stone shone back at her as he looked at the polish on his black dress shoes. She unlatched the two surface-mounted bolt locks and opened the door.

"Hope I'm not disturbing you."

Jana shook her head. "No. Come in."

"Nice place," Stone said.

"It's not, but thanks for saying."

"Are you kidding me? My place is close to a two-hour commute from here. How did you get this so close to town?"

"I'm hesitant to say," she said as she smiled.

"Sublease, huh? I bet it was lived in by an old lady who still pays 1950s rent due to rent control. Don't worry about it. I'm not going to turn you in."

"Good to know."

"Did you think about what we talked about this afternoon?"

"It's *all* I can think about. Look, Agent Stone—"

"Stone. Call me Stone."

"Okay, Stone then. I'm sorry to have reacted the way I did. It's just a lot to absorb all at once, you know?"

"If it makes you feel any better, I see that type of reaction from most of the people I recruit to work as material witnesses."

Jana slumped into the only padded seat in the tiny apartment, a cloth armchair that looked as though it had been in use since the 1970s.

"A material witness. You want me to spy on my employer and then testify in open court against, what? Al-Qaeda?" Jana buried her face in her hands. "Are you out of your mind?"

Stone slid a bent metal kitchen chair with a torn vinyl seat in front of her and sat. "Jana." He looked at her with the eyes of a father and said, "Listen to me. In 1988, during the Afghan war against the Russians, Osama bin Laden founded the terror group Al-Qaeda. Two years later when the first Gulf War began, bin Laden got pissed off that Americans were in his homeland and began to target us. He hasn't stopped since. He went after us in

'92 when we were in Somalia to bring famine-relief supplies. In '93 he bombed the World Trade Center. A truck bomb in our military base in Riyadh in '95. In '97 he bombed our embassies in Kenya and Tanzania, then the bombing of the USS *Cole* in Yemen. And then there's 9/11. He doesn't stop, Jana. He's never going to stop. Not until we kill him, that is. The terrorist your boss is communicating with? Al-Jawary? He works for bin Laden, and now bin Laden is expanding his reach."

Jana leaned back in her chair. "What has all of this got to do with Petrolsoft?"

"That's what we need your help with. CFO Jeffrey Dima has never appeared on our watch lists before now, but once that communiqué from Al-Jawary showed up, the relationship between Al-Qaeda and an American corporation came to light and it scares us. Think about it, Jana. A global terror organization talking with an American multinational corporation. The possibilities are endless."

"Like what?"

"Like I said, we need your help in finding out what they're up to. I can tell you this. The communiqué we intercepted from Al-Jawary contained only one thing: a set of map coordinates. The coordinates all point to oil production facilities spread across the Middle East."

"Well Petrolsoft doesn't own any oil production facilities."

Stone stood and paced the floor. "That's right. But Petrolsoft is a software corporation that's primary focus is software used in the oil and gas industry. And Petrolsoft also sells refining and pumping equipment."

"Well sure, everyone knows that. We power the software that makes the oil and gas industry run. That's not a crime."

"Selling software and industrial equipment is not a crime,

communicating with a terror organization is."

"So you want me to what? Gather information right out from under their noses? If half of what you're saying is true, and Petrolsoft is somehow involved with Al-Qaeda, and they catch me spying on them, what do you think they're going to do to me? I'll tell you what they're going to do. After they've had their fun, they'd probably smash my fingers with a hammer, wouldn't they?"

"You'll be under twenty-four-hour surveillance. We'll be close by at all times. Nothing like that is going to happen." He walked closer. "If they are planning something big, we have to stop them. If you don't help us and they pull off an attack, you'll always blame yourself for not having stopped it. It'll be something you'll regret for the rest of your life."

Then it struck her, *her grandpa*. Stone was a much younger version of her grandpa. "You sound like my grandfather. He always told me to never do anything I'm going to regret for the rest of my life."

"A wise man."

"A great man," she said with a smile.

"Work with us, Jana."

"I'm not sure if I like you, or if I want to kill you." She exhaled. "All right. I'm in. What do you want me to do?"

"Access. You need log-in access to the highest levels of the company intranet. We have to see what they're up to. We know something is going on, but it will be your job to find out what, and fast." He reached in his coat pocket and pulled out a handwritten slip of paper. "Here, this is my cell. Call or text me anytime, day or night. And don't think you're going to wake up Mrs. Chuck Stone because there isn't one. She came to her senses and finally left me. Another thing, if you're in trouble, you call that number and ask for Lincoln. You ask for Lincoln because there is no Lincoln, understand?"

"Yeah, I get it. And where will you be? When I'm at work, I mean."

"I'll be close. My people will be all over the place. If you get afraid someone is tailing you, you call. Likelihood is that it's one of my guys, but call nonetheless. Send me text messages as you see fit. Anything you discover, you text me. But the moment you send the text, delete it from your phone, got it? Do you have that business jacket you were wearing today?"

"Yeah, what about it?"

"Grab it for me."

Jana gave him a quizzical look but opened a bureau where her hanging clothes were kept, jammed against one another. She pulled the jacket from the hanger and handed it to him.

He put on reading glasses and inspected the jacket's left shoulder. "Here," he said as he peeled off the nearly invisible tracking device. "Stick this to whatever you're wearing each day. We can track your location that way."

"What? You've been tracking me? How did you get that thing on my . . ." But as the thoughts trailed forward, Jana remembered that morning. "Is that why you put your arm around me?"

"And take this," he said as he handed her a piece of what looked like clear vellum. Attached to the reflective plastic was a flat, translucent strip about three inches long, one-quarter of an inch across, and about as thick as a piece of card stock. "It's a microphone. Peel it off the vellum and stick it to your clothing, somewhere it won't be noticed. We'll be able to hear everything going on."

"This thing is a mic?" Jana shook her head as she held the paper-thin microphone to the light. "When I headed out the door this morning, everything was so normal. Now I'm wearing a wire and walking into a pit of terrorists."

He smiled and Jana instantly felt better, as if confidence oozing from his pores had embedded into her.

"Agent Stone—"

"Just Stone. Call me Stone."

"How much danger do you think I'm putting myself in?"

Agent Stone walked toward the door. "I don't bullshit, Jana. Sorry for the language. At this point, we have no idea what we're dealing with. But if your boss is involved with Al-Jawary, you could be putting yourself in harm's way."

She crossed her arms and rubbed the goosebumps forming on them.

"Hey," he said with a tiny smile, "this is important, really important. If it wasn't, I wouldn't ask you to do this. Everything is going to be fine, Jana." He turned the door handle and left.

Jana slumped onto the armchair. "It's the eyes. That's what seems so familiar about him. He's got grandpa's eyes."

9

To Move Money

Jana's mind swirled with questions as she walked to the office the next morning. The meeting with Agent Stone had been disturbing and exhilarating all at the same time. The danger of what she might have to do scared her, but it was the accompanying adrenaline rush that surprised her.

Growing up on the farm in Tennessee, she had become accustomed to such different surroundings. Sitting on her grandfather's lap as a child while they ate supper on the porch, helping her grandmother cook, and riding the tractor. But by the time she was in her teens, Jana knew the farm was not in her blood. She loved her grandparents dearly, and the farm would always hold a special place in her heart, but she knew her destiny lay elsewhere.

And something else boiled inside her, a recurring thought that one day she would go through a series of trials, trials designed to test her, and the notion was frightening. Where these feelings came from she did not know, but perhaps having lost her parents at such an early age stirred up the perfect undercurrent of drama that set the stage for things to come. Whatever was bubbling inside made her realize an adrenaline junkie was buried beneath her cool, proper exterior. But it was more than that. She also had the feeling that she was meant for something important, and being involved in this case fit the bill.

At the end of her junior year in high school, her application to Georgetown University came as a shock to her grandfather. He had hoped she would stay nearby, perhaps majoring in agricultural sciences. With his wife of fifty-two years, and only child resting quietly in the cemetery of the First Baptist Church just a mile from the farm, the gentle man had always hoped he could pass the land to Jana. But the land was something that needed tending, something that required full-time attention, and in his estimation, it was not in Jana's heart.

So it was with crinkled eyes and a crooked smile that he hugged Jana goodbye just before she drove away to begin undergraduate studies. He died during the second semester of Jana's freshman year. As far as having family was now concerned, Jana was alone.

Back in Manhattan, she approached the reflective glass doors of the headquarters of Petrolsoft Corporation and stopped to look up at the building, silhouetted in brilliant morning light. "No backing out now," she said.

By the time she got to her desk, her nerves were already getting the best of her. "Miss Baker?" she heard from Rune Dima's office.

"Coming, sir." Jana dropped her purse on the desk and went in.

The CFO, Jeffrey Dima, who was standing behind Rune, looked her up and down. Jana saw that his eyes stopped and held at her chest. "You look very nice this morning, Miss Baker," Jeffrey said. Jana felt a slight twinge of repulsion. *Really?* she thought. *Look me in the eye. I'm up here, you prick.* But, "Thank you, sir," was all that she said.

"We've got another assignment for you," Rune said. "You had a minor in finance, correct? And a Series 7 stock broker's license."

"Yes, sir."

"Well, it's time for a crash course in banking and investing one-oh-one. Each morning, we'll hand you a spreadsheet. On this spreadsheet will be a list of financial transfers to be made that day. You will transfer money from our various bank accounts and place the investments in hedge funds you have researched for us. The reasons we are doing this are complex, so I won't bore you with those. But we've set you up as an authorized signatory with our different financial institutions for this purpose. Jeffrey here will give you the details, but essentially you'll be transferring funds from one place to another so the hedge managers can invest our money. You think you can handle that?"

"Certainly. But, sir? I hope you don't mind me asking, but isn't this normally the kind of thing done in Petrolsoft's finance and accounting group?"

"Typically, yes. But don't worry about that right now. In fact, it would be best if you didn't mention your work to them. They might get the wrong idea. In fact, Miss Baker, what we're doing, these investments, everything is to be treated with utmost confidentiality. If the information about what we're investing in gets leaked, the Securities and Exchange Commission might construe it as passing corporate secrets, insider trading, okay? I'd hate to see you get into trouble. It's critical that we not break the trust."

"It's not a problem, sir."

"That will be all, Miss Baker."

Jana retreated toward her desk and shut the door as she left. *Keep this information confidential? Not break the trust? The first thing I'm going to do is break the trust.* She went to the women's room, found the first open stall, and sent a text to Agent Stone.

10

Billions at Stake

Stone's reply to Jana's text message informing him of Petrolsoft's planned investments was brief.

There's a J. C. Penney inside Manhattan Mall, two blocks north on W. Thirty-Second at Avenue of the Americas. Look for me. There, you'll receive further instructions.

Meet the FBI guy at Penney's? Sure, she thought. *Pass information that violates insider trading laws? Lose my Series 7 license, be barred from working in finance ever again? Just an average day in Manhattan.*

Later that day when Jana arrived at the mall, she walked into the wide entrance of J. C. Penney but had no idea what to do next.

"This guy is going to give me a nervous breakdown. There's too many things to keep up with," she said, and then recalled some of the advice Stone had given her. "Don't be followed, don't let anyone know you are snooping the corporate network." She put her hands on her hips. "Don't get killed by the nice terrorists."

From across the store, Jana saw Agent Stone standing on the far side of the makeup counter. He made eye contact, then turned away and walked deeper into the store. Jana followed and found him in the men's department looking at dress shirts.

"Don't come too close," he warned. "Don't make eye contact. Just stay on the other side of this display and we can talk. So what have you learned?"

"In a day?" Jana said. "Stone, this isn't a game of Monopoly. You've got to give me more time."

"The clock is ticking, Miss Baker."

"Ticking? Ticking to what?"

"That's just it, we don't know. That's where you come in. You are our eyes." He glanced at her ever so briefly. "The director sends his regards, by the way."

"The director of the FBI? You must be joking. Why would he know about me?"

"Jana, I don't want to scare you—"

"Now you *are* scaring me. What are you talking about?"

Stone exhaled and pulled a shirt off the shelf, then held it up to his chest. "Chatter has escalated, exponentially. NSA, Miss Baker. The National Security Agency is tracking a number of communication threads. Apparently, bin Laden has Al-Jawary on the move. There's a huge influx in the number of communications going back and forth between terror cell members."

Jana shook her head. "Stone, pretend for a moment I don't know anything about terror cells, which shouldn't be hard for you to imagine, and spell it out for me. What does that mean?"

"It means Al-Jawary's terror cell is talking to each other with greater and greater frequency. That only happens as a terror group gets close to launching whatever strike they have planned. Think of it this way. Did you ever plan to go on a weekend trip with a friend? And in the days that lead up to the trip, you two talk several times, then there's several more phone calls back and forth to work out the last-minute details? The terrorists are no different. The timetable is closing, Jana. We have to move."

"I don't even have log-in access to anything on the network that could help. But, I'll say this, the CEO is acting strangely."

"How so?"

"Well," Jana said, "he and that prick CFO of his."

"Prick? Very nice. Go on."

"They've been together behind closed doors a lot. Got me researching a bunch of hedge funds."

"Hedge funds? What kind of hedge funds?"

"That's just it. Everything we were taught about investing at Georgetown always pointed to *diversification* of a portfolio. But these idiots are having me identify the top hedge funds globally that invest with a heavy weighting in oil-related stocks."

"We thought the amount of investing was strange. Well," Stone replied, "the company builds software for the oil and gas industry—maybe they're just investing in their segment."

"It's idiotic from an investment-portfolio standpoint. They're committing massive resources to it. After I get done, they'll have over sixty-two percent of their liquidity tied up in the same sector."

"Wait, how much money are we talking about here?"

"About forty-five *billion* dollars out of a sixty-billion-dollar portfolio. It's a bad idea."

"Unless . . . unless they have insider information. Insider information that tells them the oil market is going to go up."

"Is that why we're here? To arrest them on some Insider Trading Sanctions Act violation?"

"Of course not. The SEC would do that. But if Petrolsoft is making a forty-five-billion-dollar bet on the oil market, something is wrong. Let's think this through. We can assume your bosses, Rune and Jeffrey Dima, wouldn't make a bet that big unless they were sure. They'd have to have insider information, something about the oil futures market. I'm betting he—"

"Stone," Jana interrupted. "We need to consider the tie-in to Al-Qaeda's own Abu Adim Al-Jawary."

Agent Stone grinned.

"What are you laughing at?" Jana said.

"You. Listen to yourself. When we first talked, you were a million miles away from the idea of being involved in breaking this terror cell. And now you sound like me. You sound like a fed."

"All right, so maybe it excites me. Maybe I didn't count on the adrenaline rush. But you're changing the subject."

"By all means," Stone said as he laughed, "please continue, Agent Baker."

"Oh, shut up. And that's another thing. I figured out why I find you so easy to talk to."

"I'm easy to talk to? Tell that to my ex-wife. But tell me, why am I easy to talk to?"

"Because you remind me of my grandfather."

"Now I'm offended," Stone said, but his grin said he didn't mean it.

"I'm right, aren't I?" Jana continued. "To consider this investment and the possible payoff as being tied in to Al-Qaeda. Look, Stone, if they make a pile of money, doesn't that mean they could fund terror operations or something?"

"Yes it does, Miss Baker. But I think I've created a monster."

"They're going to have me transfer more money and make more investments, so this thing is growing. But there's something I need from you. I want the background on the CFO. I'm getting increasingly nervous around him."

"Jeffrey Dima, yes. I'm not surprised by that."

"And why is that?"

"Lady killer, a real slimeball. Our workup suggests he sees himself as a playboy, thinks every woman is interested in him."

"Yeah, well not me," Jana said. "He's good looking, yes, but he makes me sick. Every time I look up, he's staring at me. Thinks he's so clever too. He makes a habit of walking right up to my desk to tell me something when all he's really trying to do is look down my blouse. He's in this investment scheme up to his eyeballs. He and Rune are plotting this together."

"I do have one other piece of bad news to deliver," Stone said.

"Which is?"

"The wire you're wearing, we're not picking anything up from it."

"It's broken?"

"No, it's working fine. But whenever you're inside your office, there's interference and it prevents us from hearing anything. It's when you go down into the lobby or leave the office that we can hear clearly. We've got some electronics experts coming in to discuss it. There may be eavesdropping countermeasure devices in place in the building. Don't let it bother you right now, just focus on your job."

"Easy for you to say," she said.

Agent Stone looked at his watch. "We've spent too much time talking already. You need to get back. Bring me a list of all the hedge funds they want to invest in. And make a copy of all the investments you make and through which financial institutions. We need account numbers."

"I can do better than that," Jana replied. "They're setting me up as a signatory on the accounts so I can move funds and make the purchases myself. I'll have log-in access to those accounts, so I can give you those."

"Here," he said as he handed a USB thumb drive across the display rack. "Download the data onto this. Attached to the side is Velcro. Tomorrow at lunch, come to the food court here in the mall. I'll be at a table. Look around until you find me, but don't approach me. Order something to eat and when you see me get up to leave, sit at that table. Underneath the table you'll be able to feel the other side of the Velcro. Press the thumb drive to it. One of my guys will retrieve it after you've gone. And Jana, the stakes are getting higher. Watch your ass."

She smirked. "Won't have to. Jeffrey Dima is watching it for me."

11

The Time is Now

As the days ticked by, Jana grew warier of Jeffrey Dima. His advances were becoming less subtle. And with the workaholic culture of the company, the hours were exhausting. Jana had been able to supply Stone with log-in information to each hedge fund she was directing investments toward, and the FBI was pleased. It gave them unfettered access into the accounts to see the exact transactions and balances. The evidence was piling up. However, nothing criminal had yet been detected. The Securities and Exchange Commission was wired in tightly to the case. The assumption was that Petrolsoft, and more specifically, Jeffrey and Rune Dima, were involved in insider trading; hardly the type of felony Agent Stone was looking for. But thus far not even the SEC had been able to ascertain the source of insider information, nor specifically what information they had in the first place. And that was no surprise. The SEC, a highly underfunded branch of the federal government, had just a single resource that was even aware of the potential issue, an investigator named John Cameron.

Jana herself began to worry that if this investigation did not pan out, she'd eventually be caught and fired for her actions. Or worse, they might kill her. Still, Agent Stone knew more was happening than they were able to yet see. The communication from Al-Qaeda leader, Abu Adim Al-Jawary, was cryptic to say the least. The NSA decoded the transmission with a decryption hash that was originally written by Section Chief William "Uncle Bill" Tarleton. The man had become a legend at NSA. Even the current director of the FBI, Steven Latent, who himself was being kept apprised of the Petrolsoft investigation, had vouched on more than one occasion for Uncle Bill. "I've known him since undergrad," Director Latent had said. "If he says he intercepted a transmission from a known terror cell, then the threat is real." And now, Agent Stone was getting daily threat assessments from Uncle Bill himself. Director Latent had told him, "If Bill is involved directly, this is more than a big deal. Find the missing pieces to this puzzle, Stone, or we're going to have a problem on our hands."

What was still puzzling to Stone was the content of the original encrypted message that NSA had intercepted. The communication included nothing but coordinates to points on a map. To Agent Stone's pleasure, at least he knew they were on the right track. The coordinates pointed to the exact locations of oil and gas refineries scattered throughout the Middle East. Why Al-Qaeda would want to point to those locations was anyone's guess. But, Stone was not going to give up until he found out. He was very concerned for Jana's safety, but she was the only person in the world that could gain access into the Petrolsoft corporate network.

Jana too, had grown fond of him. When they communicated, Stone felt like he was listening to his daughter. To his thinking, she was as bright a young woman as he had ever known. And she had that edge to her, the kind of edge that enabled her to see details others missed. It was a dogged determination that reminded him of his trainee days at the FBI's training facility on the Marine Corps base at Quantico. And the more he thought about it, the more he realized Jana had what it took to do his job. She was uncanny. And the one thing she had that so many other FBI applicants did not was that slight edge of a thrill-seeker. She was exhilarated by what she was doing as an undercover informant and it was obvious. But, she was going to have to take it to the next level. She was going to have to steal the log-in for either Rune or Jeffrey Dima's personal laptop, and she was going to have to do it right now.

12

Access Required

Jana's phone vibrated with an incoming text message. She lowered it to her lap so that the phone's screen could not be seen by anyone else in the office.

Must get access to one of their laptops. We're running out of time. Delete this message immediately.

"Yeah, no kidding," Jana mumbled as she deleted the message. Then a voice startled her.

"Your boyfriend?" Jeffrey Dima said as he walked closer and leaned over Jana's desk.

"What? Oh, no. I don't have a boyfriend." But as soon as the words left her mouth, she regretted divulging that fact to Jeffrey.

"No boyfriend? A beautiful girl like you? What a shame. And you're new in town, right? Well, I can show you around, if you know what I mean."

The smell of his aftershave was enough to curl her stomach and Jana wanted to vomit. Several questions went through her mind. *Was he attractive? Certainly. Did he dress well? Definitely. Was he a slimeball? Without a doubt.*

"Yes, I know exactly what you mean." Her tone had been more

abrupt than she'd intended

"So hostile, Miss Baker. Really, you should give me a chance. I'm an acquired taste."

A taste of what? Jana thought. "Sorry, Mr. Dima. I didn't mean to be so short with you. I just—"

"You were just about to say that since you hurt my feelings, you'd be glad to join me for a drink after work today. After all, it's Friday."

"Ah, I don't know about that."

"I'll show you the big city."

Jana sized him up a moment and came to the realization that if she were to steal log-in access to his laptop, she'd better get close to him. "I'm not the young fawn you think I am, Mr. Dima."

"Jeffrey. Please, call me Jeffrey. And not the young fawn? Good, I like that."

Jana's mind raced forward. *What are you? Like, thirty-eight years old? You are sixteen years older than I am. Not to mention that I can see you coming from a mile away, and I know exactly what that look in your eye means. So keep your fly zipped, asshole.* But still, this might be the one chance she had at stealing his passcode.

"I'll think about it," she said with a little grin.

"She'll think about it," Jeffrey said as he leaned away from the desk and walked toward his office. As he got to the door, he turned back and flashed his freshly whitened teeth at her. Set against the coal black of his hair and eyes, they looked fluorescent.

As Jana got back to work, she logged into another hedge fund account and began inputting wire transfer instructions for another large investment in an oil-heavy portfolio. The phone vibrated again. It was Stone.

Meet at usual place—priority is escalating.

49

Priority is escalating? Jana thought. *What now? They want me to scale the outside of the building with suction cups attached to my hands and feet?* But she knew that if Agent Stone thought the situation was worsening, it was serious.

13

A Shocking Revelation

"No," Stone said to Jana. "Absolutely not. I don't want you within ten feet of that thug."

"Why?" Jana said. "Look, Stone, you know I can't stand the guy. But it might be my only way to find out what his username and password are. If I go out with him, I might be able to get a look at his files."

"It's out of the question."

Jana looked across the wide-open expanse of the J. C. Penney men's section. "What's wrong?"

Stone looked down, then leveled serious eyes at her and shook his head.

"Come on, Stone. Spit it out. There's something you're not telling me."

"Background check on Jeffrey Dima."

"What about it?"

"I didn't want to say anything earlier. I thought that even with what we found in his past, you were safe because you were just working in the same office as him. But going out with him? Even with my team close by, it's not safe."

"What about his background check?"

"He's been accused on three separate occasions of using Rohypnol on young women. Never convicted, but the pattern is there. It's not safe for you to be with him, Jana. You are my responsibility."

Jana knew what Rohypnol was, a prescription drug often used to perpetrate sexual assaults on women. But the fact remained, no one knew what the terrorists were truly up to and she was the only person that was in a position to find out. *Someone has to stop this attack, whatever it might be. Someone has to stand in the gap—the gap between us and them.* "Aren't you getting a little bit too fatherly?"

"Too . . . oh give me a break. I'm looking out for the safety of my number one witness. I've been a federal agent for longer than you've been alive. I know what I'm talking about."

"I'm a big girl and can take care of myself. But thanks, Dad."

Stone smirked at the reference to his age. "Look, Jana, if these guys are involved with terrorists, you have no idea what they're capable of. Ever heard of rendition? You know, a form of kidnapping where the person gets snatched off the street so fast you can't even react? By the time we caught up to you, it would be too late."

"Tell me why you said the case had escalated in priority. And, Stone, don't leave anything out. I know you've been hiding other things from me. I'm in this up to my ears and I want to know the truth."

Stone's shoulders slumped. "We've identified each of the map coordinates sent in the original transmission. As you know, they point to oil-production facilities all over the Middle East. But not every oil facility in those regions is included in the list. These are all either American-owned oil facilities, or those owned by one of our allies. Jana, we don't know what that means. But the fact that NSA is detecting such a huge increase in chatter between bin Laden's Al-Qaeda terror cells tells us an attack is imminent. Whatever is being planned is getting close."

"I can see it in your eyes, Stone. You're still holding back. I said spit it out."

"Remember the guy I told you about at NSA? The one I said that FBI Director Steven Latent knew personally? Well, "Uncle Bill" intercepted a particularly disturbing communiqué this morning." He looked down then said, "*Your name*, Jana. Your name was mentioned in a communiqué that was sent from Abu Adim Al-Jawary. He knows who you are."

Jana pulled away. "Why the hell would a terrorist in the Middle East know who I am?"

"It would be part of their mode of operation. Once whatever they have planned gets rolling, they'll want to erase their tracks."

"Erase their tracks?" But as the thought played forward in Jana's mind, she understood what he meant. The terrorists would kill her.

14

Simpler Times

The walk back to the office was not an easy one. The growling in her stomach had stopped, but was now replaced with a feeling of vulnerability. *A senior leader in one of the most feared terrorist organizations in the world knows who I am.* And Jana knew, if the terrorists knew her identity, they probably know far more about her than that, like where she lived. Suddenly, just the thought of getting on the train for the commute home frightened her. *What if they're watching me right now? No, Stone would know. He's got eyes on me right now, right? I mean, surely some pair of FBI eyes is always nearby.*

She clutched her purse with both hands and scanned in all directions. How would she ever spot someone following her? The streets of New York are filled with humanity at this hour. It would be like finding a needle in a stack of needles. Not to mention the fact that even if she scanned the faces all around her, looking for those of Middle Eastern descent, that wouldn't help much either. New York is a melting pot—every race and skin tone is here. *Racial profiling,* Jana thought. *This is how it starts. The paranoia creeps in and you start looking for that stereotypical picture of what you think a terrorist would look like.* Darker skin, black hair, black eyes, a thick, unkempt black beard, and perhaps wearing a thawb, a commonly worn ankle-length garment, similar to a robe, with long sleeves. It was all starting to sound like something out of a Hollywood movie.

Jana shivered. Her own mind was playing tricks on her and it wouldn't be wise to allow the racism and paranoia building in her veins to continue. As she speed-walked down the sidewalk, she stopped in the doorway of a small neighborhood market to extract herself from the full-paced walkers all around her, then pulled out her phone. She typed out a text message to Agent Stone.

I want a weapon, and I want to be trained how to use it. And, Dad? I'm not asking.

She sent the text and then deleted it from her list of messages. *Calling him dad; I'm sure he's going to just love that one,* she thought as a smile eased onto her face. *Not to mention me demanding a weapon.*

Once back in the office, Jana found she had trouble concentrating. She logged in to another brokerage account, this one an offshore account located in the Cayman Islands, and shook her head. *Offshore, red flag for the SEC. Even if I stop these terrorists, I'm going to lose my broker's license.* She discreetly placed the thumb drive into a USB port on the laptop and recorded the financial transaction complete with date, time, amounts, account numbers, and the institutions involved. She closed her eyes and her thoughts wandered.

In her mind's eye, she found herself back in the second grade, back in the principal's office, the sheriff's deputy telling her that her mother had died. The swirl of emotions that came with the news was overwhelming. That night, she slept at her teacher's

55

house, and in the morning woke to the smell of freshly cooked waffles. When she went toward the sound of Miss Hancock's voice, she found that her own grandfather was sitting at the table in the eat-in kitchen with a cup of coffee in his hand, and her grandmother was hovering over Miss Hancock, ladling scrambled eggs onto her plate. Jana knew she would go live with them on their farm in rural Tennessee.

She had always loved the farm, and she truly loved her grandparents, but the thought of leaving everything she knew was frightening.

It had been only a month later that her grandmother, too, died. From that point on, it was just Jana and Grandpa. He had become her whole world. Some of the best times in her childhood were suppers spent with her grandfather as they ate on the porch. When she was little, she would sit in his lap as he reached around her to cut her food. Then when she was bigger, they still enjoyed eating on the porch and watching the sun as it dipped below the tree line across the expanse of farmland, then set.

The sun's amber glow was still strong in her memory. And now as an adult, Jana longed for those days, for their simplicity, their honesty, and the love she felt.

Jana's world had changed so much since then and she wondered how everything had gotten so confusing. The stress inside her was building toward eventual eruption, and Jana wondered how much longer she could keep this up. She removed the thumb drive from the laptop and tucked it just inside her bra, obscured from view.

"What are you up to, Jana?" came a voice. She startled, then found Jeffrey Dima staring at her. *Did he see?* she thought as her heart leapt into her mouth.

"Oh, nothing. Just working on your project." She prayed that answer would suffice.

He walked to her desk and his eyes wandered to what pleased them. "I think you should give me another chance."

"And why is that?"

"I'm not such a bad guy."

"That's not what I hear."

"You've been asking around about me?" he said through a pearly white smile. "See, I'm not so bad. Come on, admit it. You're attracted to me."

"I'll admit nothing of the kind." It was a flirtatious answer and one Jana would later parlay into accepting his advances. But, she had to get certain things organized before she would willingly set foot in this sleazeball's apartment.

"Come on, this Saturday night. I'll cook you a meal you won't believe."

"Jeffrey, we're coworkers. This can never happen."

"It's America, Jana. Anything can happen. It's a date then."

Jana processed the situation. She didn't have much time to prepare, but then again, with the timetable on the terror attack closing down, she had to act as quickly as possible.

"No," she said with innocence in her eyes.

"No?"

"I'm busy Saturday. Make it Friday and I'll think about it."

His smile widened and his eyes again wandered across her form. Although Jana was repulsed, she made no outward signs of it.

Now, it was time to give Agent Stone a critical assignment, one that would prepare her for Friday night.

15

The Firing Range

"I can't believe you talked me into this," Agent Stone said to Jana as he positioned noise-canceling earmuffs over his ears. "Now, just like I told you. Keep the weapon pointed downrange at all times. That means the barrel never faces any direction other than downrange. Got it?"

The sounds of gunfire coming from the shooting lanes next to them were so loud that to Jana they sounded like cannons. She took a deep breath and adjusted her safety glasses.

"Keep the gun pointed downrange at all times, check."

"It's not a joke, Miss Baker. This is a Walther PPK .380-caliber firearm. It would kill either one of us in a matter of seconds."

The look in Stone's eyes had changed. She was no longer looking into the eyes of her grandfather. He was serious, deadly serious.

"Whenever you put a hand on this weapon, I want you to picture in your mind that it is firing one time every second."

"Why is that?" Jana said.

"Because if the gun is firing once per second, you will keep it pointed in a safe direction."

She took the weapon in both hands and extended her arms. Stone reached around her from behind and put his hands on her wrists to steady them. "With this weapon, you want to keep the thumb on your left hand tucked on the side. Don't let it drape behind the gun. If you do, it could get popped very hard by the action of the gun when it fires. Now, just pull the trigger and be prepared for the gun to pop in your hand."

Although she startled after the first round was fired, after that, she settled into it. They spent over an hour at the FBI's shooting range, and by the time it was over, Jana felt confident.

Stone said, "You did really, really well. And you never shot a pistol before? I've got to say, I'm impressed. I didn't do that well my first time out."

"Stone, I know shooting is serious business, but I had fun. Thank you for teaching me. Having a weapon is going to make me feel a little more comfortable."

"Just don't let your guard down. And always, always remember, double tap, center mass, then one to the head."

The words reverberated in her head. She hoped she would never have to use them.

16

Determination of Spirit

In the men's department of J. C. Penney, Agent Stone yelled. "You're going to do what?"

A woman holding up a business suit to her husband turned and stared.

"You heard me," Jana replied. "Stone, you and I both know that time is running out. Uncle Bill said it himself. Whatever the terrorists are planning is about to happen, and we've got to stop it."

"Jana, listen to me. You can't go into that penthouse apartment with him. You're not dealing with some average schmuck from Brooklyn. This guy is sending up red flags everywhere we look. In fact, when we pulled his fingerprints off a restaurant wine glass, we found no match."

"So what. Are every human being's prints in the database?"

"Everyone who has a New York state driver's license has prints in the database, yes. *He* has a New York license, yet no prints exist for him. Don't you find that a bit strange?" The sarcasm hung thick. "That means we're dealing with a false identity. But it's much worse than that. Under his current identity of Jeffrey Dima, he has been brought in for questioning by the NYPD Special Victims Unit to be interrogated about the three incidents, the one's where he was accused of using Rohypnol on young women. No charges were ever filed in those cases due to lack of evidence, but my point is, there's still no prints in the database. That means somehow they've been erased. We're talking about heavy hitters here. You could get really hurt."

"I can take care of myself."

Stone placed his hands on his hips and leveled a stern look. "That's what those other three young women would have said before he assaulted them. It's not safe, Jana, and I don't want you doing this."

"It's my safety and my decision. The plan is simple. All you have to do is get me a prescription of Rohypnol. I'll handle the rest."

"I still think you're crazy, and I don't want to see you get hurt. We might have an imminent terrorist threat, but that doesn't mean I'm willing to let you sacrifice yourself."

Jana walked closer to him. When she looked into his eyes, she saw emotions forming within. "Stone, what's going on?"

Agent Stone turned his back to prevent her from seeing his face.

"Nothing."

"There's something going on."

He rubbed his eyes. "She was fifteen years old."

Jana tilted her head. "Who? Who was fifteen years old?"

Stone swallowed. "In high school. My girlfriend, her name was Alyssa. We were both fifteen. Her nude body was found in a dumpster a few days later. She had been murdered." He turned to face her and she could see the glistening in his eyes. "They threw her away like she was an object to be used, then discarded."

Jana did not know what to say and the silence punctuated Stone's hidden grief.

"I'm sorry," was the best she could muster. "That's what led you to law enforcement, wasn't it? To a career as a federal agent. And now you think the same thing is going to happen to me? Is that what this is about?"

"Yes," he whispered. "I feel responsible for you in the same way I felt responsible for Alyssa. I don't want to see anything happen to you."

"Having lost my own father at the age of two, I've never had anyone say that to me. But, Stone, look at me. I'm not going to get hurt, all right? I'll wear a wire and you'll be listening; you and the other agents. If you hear anything going wrong . . ."

"I know, I know. But Jana, if he finds that wire device on you, he could kill you before we would even know something was up. What you are about to do is extremely dangerous, don't forget that. Don't let your guard down for a moment."

Jana smiled and tension eased from his shoulders. "I won't, Dad."

Stone laughed. "I still don't know how you are going to know where his supply is. If you don't locate it first, he could drug you, and you wouldn't even be able to alert us that there was a problem."

"Just leave that to me," Jana said.

17

Early Morning Fear

With all the tension of her situation, Jana's emotions bubbled to the surface. Exhaustion had overtaken her, but she could not fall asleep. The realization that Agent Stone thought of her like a daughter swirled with the feelings of exhaustion as Jana finally drifted off, thinking back to her childhood. Flashes of memories formed into a dream, a dream of Jana's youth. She found herself again catapulted back to the farm, a place that had become the only stability in the life of a young child whose parents had died. It was supper time and she was seated in her grandfather's lap on the porch. His warm arms reached around her, a fork in one hand, a knife in the other. He squeezed his arms to hug her at the same time he cut into the country fried steak on Jana's plate in front of them. He put the knife down and lifted the fork to hold the first bite of food in front of Jana's little mouth. His free hand found its way to her tiny rib cage and he tickled her. Jana giggled and he said, "Come on, sweet pea. Time to eat. Why are you not eating?" But Jana laughed and laughed at his touch.

"I can't eat!" she said, squirming and giggling in his lap.

"Why not, sweet pea? Come on now, grandpa says it's time to eat."

"You're tickling me!" she said, roaring with laughter that her grandpa found infectious.

While his tickling and her squirming continued, he said, "These are not the tickles. There are no tickles. Now eat your steak."

A knock on the door at 5:10 a.m. startled Jana her from the dream and back into a frightening reality, a reality in which she would place herself further into harm's way. As she rubbed her eyes, the sadness of all the loss she'd suffered in her life crashed against the backs of her eyes, like water rushing through a pipe that suddenly finds itself stopped by a valve. The back pressure was building and Jana strained to push the tears down.

She wanted to call someone; she wanted to speak to a friend. But Jana didn't have many of those. She'd always found it hard to make friends that were women. It wasn't until her junior year at Georgetown University that her roommate told her why. "They hate you because of your looks," she had said.

"What looks?" she replied. "I don't give any of the girls mean looks. I smile at everybody."

"No, they're jealous of *you*, Jana. It's your beauty, your body. They see you, then look in the mirror as they compare themselves against you. They're jealous. Then they see the guys swirling around you and it makes them feel inferior. Half of them would kill to get the attention of any one of those guys, but they're all fawning over you and the girls hate you for it."

The shock had come like a slap in the face. Jana had grown up in a very quiet, reserved farming town. Boys had always paid attention to her, but it had never gone to her head. In fact, it had never even occurred to her to consider herself superior to anyone else. Her grandfather's upbringing had taught nothing but love for other people. Jana's values had been formed during those years, years spent helping her grandpa on the farm, and at church, where he taught Sunday school. No, Jana had no one to turn to in the bleakness of the morning. No close girlfriend she could rely on, no boyfriend she considered to be a soul mate. She was alone, alone with her feelings.

With FBI agents working surveillance around the periphery of her apartment building at all hours of the day and night, she had little fear that the person knocking on the door was any type of threat. Her bare feet hit the cold wood floor and the old oak boards squeaked in protest. She tiptoed to look out the peephole. Agent Stone's scalp shined back at her, and Jana unbolted the two locks, slipped the security chain off its rail, and pulled the door open.

"Dad, it's early," she said through a grin.

As Stone walked into the cramped studio apartment, he said, "You're really going to call me that?"

"I'm just messing with you, Stone," she said, this time yawning. "Why are you here?"

"I couldn't sleep."

"Well, I could. Until now, that is."

"Sorry to wake you. Look, we have to talk about tonight. Tonight is Friday and you are about to walk into the penthouse apartment of someone who's just graced the terror watch list. And there's more you need to hear about. My surveillance team has been scoping his penthouse apartment, and there's a problem."

"Besides the fact that you think he's going to drug then sexually assault me?"

"His apartment is surrounded in mirrored glass. The surveillance team pointed a laser microphone at it."

"A laser microphone?"

"Yes, we use laser mics to listen in on conversations where we don't have a listening device planted inside. The mic focuses on a window pane, and interprets the vibrations it picks up as a conversation takes place inside. We can hear the voices that way. We have access to an office suite across the street which we've been using to surveil him. At any rate, the laser mic isn't going to work in this case." He put his hands on his hips and leaned closer to her face. "There's a stick-on composite film on the exterior of the glass, similar to the way a car window gets tinted. But this is no window tinting. This is countermeasure film. It's designed to interrupt the pattern of vibrations coming from voices inside the apartment. In short, it's designed to thwart laser mics."

"You are sounding paranoid."

His volume escalated. "Paranoid? What kind of a person puts countermeasure film against their apartment windows? I'll tell you what kind. The kind of person that wants to make sure the feds are not listening. Jana, *no one* has countermeasure film like this. It's not something you order off Amazon. Am I paranoid? Damn right I'm paranoid. The federal government pays me to be paranoid. He's got to be a much bigger terrorist than we believed. In fact, we're definitely getting a clearer picture that it's *Jeffrey* Dima, and not so much Rune Dima, that is the ringleader here. Rune may be the CEO of the company, but where these terrorist connections are concerned, Jeffrey is calling the shots."

"We went over a lot of this last night. I'm a big girl. I can take care of myself."

"You aren't getting it!" Stone blasted. "When we detected the countermeasure film, my team looked further. And they discovered something else we didn't foresee."

"And what's that?"

"Jeffrey has a maid that comes to clean up about every other day—"

"Oh no!" Jana blurted, her hands finding her face. "Not a maid!

Oh, the danger!" The sarcasm was not well received.

"You *are* like a daughter. A teenage daughter," Stone said.

"Very funny."

"We were suspicious, so we hid an electronic mic, a bug, in her cart yesterday. When she went into his apartment, the listening device transmitted and recorded *nothing*." He let the statement hang in space a moment to see if Jana would pick up on the significance. When she held up her hands, he said, "Do you know what that means? It means his apartment is equipped to jam electronic transmissions. Almost undoubtedly, he's blocking all frequencies outside of the normal cellphone range, which means you won't be able to wear a wire. Any wire you wear will be jammed. We won't be able to hear what's going on in that apartment." He shook his head. "No. You are five feet, three inches tall. He's a foot taller and seventy pounds heavier. You'd be all alone in there, and I won't allow it."

Jana looked at the ground then into his eyes. "Stone, we've talked about the dangers. I know about the Rohypnol, I have a plan, and I can take care of myself."

"Oh, can you?" Stone said as he suddenly spun Jana around by the shoulders, wrenched her arm behind her back, and placed a thick forearm around her neck in a choking position. "What about now? Can you take care of yourself now?" he said, exasperation oozing from the edges of his voice. "What are you going to do if he does this to you? Huh? If he wants to hurt you, we wouldn't know about it, and you wouldn't be able to do a thing to stop him."

"Oh, yeah?" she gurgled from under the choking pressure on her throat. "Well what if I did this?" She raised her knee into the air and slammed the edge of her bare heel into the top, right edge of his foot, impacting the dorsal lateral cutaneous nerve.

Stone recoiled and his grip abated as the shockwave of pain rocketed up his foot and into his leg. He knelt down and sat on the ground as his hands gripped the foot. "Oh shit, that hurts."

She knelt down beside him and placed a hand on his shoulder. "Stone, you think I've never taken a self-defense class? Look, I'm vulnerable, okay? But I'm not a little lamb. You and I both know this investigation is going almost nowhere. Right now, all we have are records of financial transactions. There's no crime there. You told me earlier, it's the *reason* for the investments that is at question, and the fact that there's a known terror connection."

"Okay, let's say you are able to get into his apartment, pull off the plan we've discussed, then you are able to rifle through his laptop and we find clues. What then? Do you realize you might have to testify in open court against him and Rune Dima, against Al-Qaeda itself? You'd have to enter the witness protection program. You'd have to disappear from your life."

They both stood. "What life? Stone, I have very few friends, and the ones I do have aren't even there for me. I have no family, and my life here in Manhattan just started. If anyone is in a good position to start their life over, it's me. I'm ready, and I'm not backing down from this."

"You've got guts, kid, and guts is enough. Where is this chip on your shoulder coming from? What is it you think you have to prove to somebody?"

"Not to somebody, Stone, to me. I can't name one thing I've ever done in my life that's truly important. Most people never get this opportunity. I'm going to prove to myself that I can do this."

"One tough kid," Stone said with a half smile. The phone in his pocket vibrated. "Stone," he said into it. "Who? Who's coming up here?" Stone's right hand found the firearm on his hip as though a magnet had attracted it there. "Okay, get everybody on alert. I want three units out of their position and into the stairwell. Do it now."

"What's going on?" Jana said as she backed away.

"Get behind the bed. Lay on the ground. Someone's coming up."

"At this hour?" Jana said.

Stone held his hand on his weapon and peered out the peephole in the door. A man wearing a ball cap came into view, holding a long, tall, white box, then glanced at a clipboard as if confirming he was at the correct address. Stone stepped aside, fearing the box might contain a weapon—he did not want to be in the line of fire. He removed his Glock from its holster. The doorbell rang and Stone held a finger to his lips, signaling Jana to stay quiet. After a moment, the bell rang again. Stone waited, then heard footsteps walking away from the door. He glanced out the peephole to find the hallway empty. He opened the door and glanced in either direction. The white box had been leaned against the door frame.

"Flowers," Jana said as she peered over the bed. "Looks like a box of flowers."

"Don't touch it," Stone said as he held a hand up.

"Stone, give me a break. You think the terrorists are going to drop off a bomb at my house? It's flowers, for God's sake." Jana picked the featherweight box off the floor and opened it. Inside lay a single, long-stem, white rose nestled in white tissue paper. "See? I told you. Try not to be so paranoid."

"No card? A white rose? What's that supposed to mean?"

"Come on, Stone. Don't you know anything about women?"

"Of course I do, but my ex-wife would beg to differ."

"A white rose symbolizes new beginnings, or it can mean *thinking of you*."

"It's from the slimeball, isn't it?"

Jana nodded. "Yeah, he's thinking of me; thinking of separating me from my panties, that is."

"Nice," Stone said.

"Come on, Dad. I'm going to his place tonight and you know it. Now, did you bring what I asked you to bring?"

"Yes, dammit. Here it is." He handed her a prescription bottle. "Rohypnol, just like you wanted. And here," he said as he opened an envelope and withdrew a thin square of paper, about two inches across.

"What's this?" Jana said as she held it to the light.

"It's like litmus paper, only this type is made to detect the presence of Rohypnol. Hide this on your person and be sure you discreetly dip it into anything you drink. If it detects the drug, it will turn pink." He wagged a finger in her face. "Don't underestimate this guy, Jana. He's bad news. Don't drink anything unless you've tested it first."

"Really? Well what if he puts it in my food?"

Stone rubbed his temples. "You're going to give me a heart attack. And don't have more than one alcoholic drink. You'll need all your faculties if you expect to pull off what you have planned."

"Yes, Dad."

18

Virus of Destruction

Office of the CEO.
Jeffrey sat in a chair in front of Rune Dima's desk and smiled.
"It's in place," he said. "The software build containing the virus was uploaded to the cloud environment servers an hour ago. It will take a little while to filter down to all the customer's systems. An admin at each location will need to first log in to their environment. After that, the virus acts like a Trojan horse. We'll have complete autonomy at that point."

"Brilliant work, Jeffrey, really. You might be a cocky son of a bitch, but I have to hand it to you, this is going to be unbelievable."

"Cocky? Oh, come on, cousin. I'm not cocky, I'm confident."

Rune shook his head and laughed. "You think you're Allah's gift to women, right? You're cocky."

Jeffrey joined in laughing. "Well, women do adore me."

"I think I'm going to puke," Rune said as he looked out the wall of windows toward an approaching thunderstorm. "What's the update on our investments? Are all the funds in place?"

"Cousin, how you doubt me. Yes, all the funds have been dispersed to banks across the globe. And eighty percent of our planned transactions have already been executed. We now own more oil futures contracts than the Saudi government."

Rune leaned forward in his chair. "How about our paper trail? After we carry out the attack, will there be any way for authorities to track this back to us?"

"You underestimate me, cousin," Jeffrey said as he stood and walked to the bank of windows. "We've set up so many shell corporations and offshore accounts, they'll never weave their way through."

Rune leveled a stern gaze. "Is that right? Then what happened to John Cameron?"

"John Cam . . . oh, you mean the Securities and Exchange Commission investigator that had a recent car accident on the turnpike?" Jeffrey said through a grin. "Is that the John Cameron you mean?"

"You killed him, didn't you?"

"Accidents happen, cousin. And what more fitting end to an investigator that had gotten too nosy. He was a liability."

"I knew it," Rune said as he squared off in front of Jeffrey. "You were careless, weren't you? The SEC had gotten suspicious. I told you to spread out your stock transactions so you wouldn't raise attention. But you wouldn't listen."

"The purchases had to be made," Jeffrey snapped. "I told that little bitch to spread her buys across the different institutional accounts slowly. But when I looked at her transactions, she had placed too many buy orders with the same institution in a row. When I confronted her about it, she started asking questions. Kept spouting off about how this purchasing practice was highly unusual."

"Is Jana Baker the only one involved in the actual transactions?"

"Yes, of course. Do you think I'm stupid?"

"So," Rune said, "the intern starts making purchases at the same institution too many times in a row and that causes a red flag to trip at the SEC. So now the Securities and Exchange Commission puts eyes on us and that puts the entire jihad in jeopardy. Why were you not monitoring her more closely? Why were you not auditing her buys two or three times a day, for that matter? In fact, what makes you think we can trust her at all? What if she is working with the SEC on this? Did you ever think of that?"

Jeffrey poked a sharp finger into his cousin's shoulder. "You hired the little cunt. You hired her and knew what we had planned. Is she working with the SEC, you ask? Not a chance. I had been watching the SEC investigator, even listening in on his office phone calls. I had him tailed. He had no contact with Jana Baker or anyone else in this company. As you well know, we have a contact inside the walls of the SEC, and he was most effective in helping me. John Cameron was the only person in the entire organization that had suspicions about Petrolsoft and now he is dead."

"So you've tied off all the loose ends? Is that what you are saying?"

"Rune, you know as well as I do that no matter what intern we hired, that person would have too much information. When we flip the switch and this operation swings into full gear, she is our one remaining liability. Are all the loose ends tied off? No, not yet."

"So you intend to kill her?"

Jeffrey smirked. "Of course, what did you think we were going to do? Just walk out of the office and let federal authorities find her and use her as a material witness against our cause? No, she cannot survive."

"You are a coldhearted son of a bitch, Jeffrey. Do you know that? When do you intend to do it?"

"We still have twenty percent of our investments to make. It's a full-time job, and she's gotten good at it. Besides, I have other plans for her."

"Other plans?" Rune said as he crossed his arms. "And what might those be?"

"She has taken a bit of a liking to me. I have invited her up to my apartment. You know, for cocktails?"

"Cocktails? You make me sick, you know that?"

"Rune, you have become too Americanized. You have lost your path from the old ways. If you and I had stayed in our homeland of Syria, you would not be speaking like this. You would be patting me on the back and laughing at the way I intend to use her. A woman, just a woman. Women are meant for one thing cousin, and you and I know what that is. It is just that you have forgotten."

"Don't tell me I've become *Americanized.*" He spat the words like venom. "I am a jihadist, and a jihadist to the core. But I am more focused than you are. I am focused on targets, governments, institutions, or people that represent all that is evil and wrong with this filthy Christian nation. You, however, believe anyone in your sight is fair game, collateral damage no matter whether they were part of our target or not. I can see the lust in your eyes. Drug her, rape her, kill her, then dispose of the body. Am I right? You know what I am starting to wonder, Jeffrey? Whether it is *you* that is the liability."

Jeffrey jammed his hands into Rune and shoved him back. "Don't get cocky with me, cousin. Al-Jawary will be none too pleased to find you are growing beyond his control, growing beyond *my* control. I'd hate for an accident to happen to you."

Rune started to launch at him, but stopped himself short. "You just get the job done, Jeffrey. Finish all of our financial transactions, tie off all the loose ends. But do it in such a way that no one knows. Now get out of my office."

19

A Tension You Can Taste

By 7:50 a.m. Jana was already seated at her desk outside the office of Rune Dima.

Agent Chuck Stone, however, sat in the coffeehouse across the street and wrung his hands. His star witness, Jana Baker, was in a situation far more dangerous than she believed. With over twenty-three years serving as a field agent, Stone had seen situations like this go bad. Jana would be walking into the Manhattan penthouse of a known terrorist, a terrorist with a history of violence against women.

NSA Section Chief William "Uncle Bill" Tarleton had called Stone ten minutes prior and explained in terse verbiage that something big was coming down, and it was coming down immanently. NSA, in coordination with CIA field operatives, had made the connection between Jeffrey and Rune Dima. Both identities were false, but their paper trails were impeccable. They'd been raised in Syria but as early teenagers relocated to the United States with their father whose work visa enabled him entry into the country. They had blended into American society even to the point of shedding their telltale accents. To Uncle Bill, both Dima men had all the markings of sleeper agents, terrorists that had been planted inside the United States at an early age.

And now that they sat in powerful positions inside an American-owned corporation, their status in society had elevated.

What that meant to Stone was that the stakes were higher. Yet proving the two were involved in a criminal act would require strong evidence, evidence he did not yet have.

FBI Agent Larry Fry walked into the corner coffee shop and said, "We've got a problem."

"Just one?" Stone said. "What is it this time?"

"Hey, don't shoot the messenger. But they just found the body of John Cameron."

"John . . . the SEC guy that's been investigating this case from their end?"

"Yes. It appears he died in a hit-and-run auto accident on the turnpike. They just pulled his body from the river."

"No wonder I haven't been able to get ahold of him. That's terrible, did he have a wife and kids?"

"Stone," Fry said, "I don't think you're getting what I'm saying. This was a hit-and-run. One witness said it looked very intentional. A black van sped up beside Cameron's car and slammed into it, forcing it through the railings and into the river. The van then sped off."

"Wait, you're thinking this was a hit? But that would mean . . . that would mean the Dima cousins are aware of the SEC investigation into their investments, and they are willing to murder for it."

"That's right."

Stone paced the floor, not even realizing he was blocking the aisle of the coffee shop, preventing customers from placing their orders.

"Let's think about this for a minute," Stone said. "Cameron said that everything he could tell about the heavy investing into the oil futures market were already red flags that Petrolsoft had some kind of insider information about the oil market that no one else knows. But as of yet, there was no evidence to indicate anything criminal. So if we play this forward and assume the Dima boys knew they were under the microscope, and they murdered him, these guys would stop at nothing. What if they found the source of their leak? Jana would have to be next. They're going to kill her. I can't endanger her life like this. I'm going to pull her out, and pull her out right now."

But no sooner had Stone removed his phone from his pocket to call Jana than Agent Fry put his hand on Stone's arm.

"The murder of Investigator John Cameron is not all the news I have." He exhaled. "I just got off the phone with the director. He and Uncle Bill Tarleton at NSA were old college roommates. They talk all the time. The director is aware of everything you and I know, and they fear this is much worse than any of us believed. This is not just a financial scheme involving insider trading. This is going to be bigger, although they still do not know what."

Stone finally stepped aside to let other customers pass. He crossed his arms and leaned in to Fry. "No shit. None of us know exactly what is about to happen. What else is it that you aren't telling me?"

"The director says we have to go through with the operation tonight. If the witness is willing, he is ordering us to send her in there. We can't pull her off the operation. I'm sorry, Chuck."

"What? I'm in charge of this field operation. The director never plays armchair quarterback with us. That girl is in danger, and she needs to be pulled out."

"Chuck, you are preaching to the choir. But remember something: Jana Baker was made well aware that she was in grave danger, and she forced the issue anyway. She insisted that she go through with tonight's operation. To tell you the truth, I think she and the director are on the same page. They both know how much is at stake and are willing to risk it."

Stone sat at the tiny round table in front of the wall of glass. He looked up at the height of the Petrolsoft building across the street. "You're an asshole, Fry. You know that?"

Fry laughed. "Yeah, but I'm your kind of asshole. So now, since we know she's going to Jeffrey Dima's penthouse tonight, what is the plan?"

Stone rubbed his eyes. "This girl is smart as hell. She came up with this entire thing on her own. It's brilliant. Risky, but brilliant. And to have the guts to go in there, into the apartment of a thug who she knows is going to try and drug her with Rohypnol. This is like watching a firefighter bolt through a wall of flame to go in and save someone."

Stone went into detail and outlined the entire operation for Agent Fry—Jana's plan on how she would avoid being drugged, how she would get her hands on the information they needed, and the fact that the apartment had electronic eavesdropping countermeasures in place.

"It's going to be like the first time a manned spacecraft orbited the far side of the moon, a complete blackout. I'm going to pull my hair out while she's in that apartment."

To lighten the tension, Fry said, "Well that won't take long," referring to Stone's receding hairline.

"If she pulls this off," Stone said, "we should have access to the entire terrorist plan without them knowing they have been compromised."

20

To Lure a Killer

Jana rubbed her eyes and squinted at the laptop monitor. Her finger traced from one side of the screen to the other in an effort to double-check herself before she executed this last trade. This was the largest investment Petrolsoft would be making into the volatile oil futures market. The thought that this might be the last trade she would make as a licensed stock broker sat heavy on her stomach. *I might be acting on behalf of the federal government in a terrorism investigation, but the only thing other employers are going to see on my resume is the word Petrolsoft.* After today, the name would become synonymous with global terrorism.

Out of the corner of her eye, she saw Jeffrey Dima lean against his office door, his arms crossed. The little grin that painted his face as he stared at her spoke volumes.

"Want me to pick you up tonight? Say, seven o'clock?"

Jana leveled sultry eyes at him and wondered if he could tell it was all an act. "Why wait?" Her thought was that if she allowed him to go back to his apartment without her, that might give him time to put his hands on his stash of Rohypnol. No, she was determined to keep him in her sight. She also thought that if she pretended to be interested in him, it might throw him off his perceived need to drug her in the first place. "It's six already.

Why don't we go for a drink? Isn't there a place at the bottom of your building?"

"Now how do you know where I live?" Jeffrey said as his grin widened and he walked to her desk.

"Oh, I know things," Jana replied with a coy look on her face.

"You know things, do you? Well what else do you know about me?"

Jana's expression flattened. "I know you have a certain reputation, with women, I mean. It's said that you make the rounds, so to speak."

"And that doesn't bother you?"

Jana looked over her shoulder to make sure no one else was nearby. "What makes you think I don't make the rounds myself?"

"My, my. We are going to have an interesting evening, aren't we? And yes, there is a place to grab a drink at the bottom of my building. The Forty-Forty Club. I'm a member. I think you'll like it."

Jana turned her attention to the laptop monitor and clicked her mouse on a button labeled "Execute Trade," then looked back at Jeffrey. "I just made the last buy. That's it, it's all done."

"Well in that case, it's happy hour. The club is just four blocks down."

21

On the Move

Across the street in the coffeehouse, Stone focused his attention on the front doors of the sprawling Petrolsoft building.

"You know we've got eight pairs of eyes trained on that building right now?" Agent Fry said. "Every exit is covered. Don't worry, we're going to see her when she walks out."

"I know," Stone said, "but our surveillance teams are not as familiar with her as I am. I could spot her a mile away."

"You taking a liking to young Miss Baker?"

"It's not like that. She's a kid. Twenty-two years old. More like a daughter."

"Come on, Stone. You know better than to allow yourself to become attached to a material witness. It could be dangerous."

Stone's eyes never left the doorway across the street as he scanned the throngs of humanity exiting the building at the close of Friday's business day. "It's not dangerous, it's smart. And it isn't something that I can control, at any rate. She's a great young woman and I don't want to see her get hurt. The fact that I'm so worried about her only increases her safety." He straightened up in his chair. "That's her. Navy blue skirt, double-breasted suit jacket."

Fry squinted in the direction of the doors. "Are you sure?"

But Stone was unabated and raised a radio to speak. "Squad two, squad two, this is Stone. Subject on the move. North entrance. She's accompanied by our target. Heading south on Madison Avenue."

"Roger that," came the terse reply. "We're on it. Mobile four, mobile five, keep your distance, but don't lose eye contact."

Stone, Fry, and the members of surveillance squad two leapt into action and walked out into the stream of people flooding the sidewalks of Madison Avenue.

Fry said, "Check the tracker. You picking up the ping?"

Stone looked at his phone and opened the FBI's secure tracking application. "Yeah, I've got her. She's about fifty yards ahead of us. Dammit, I've lost visual though. Do you see her?"

"Relax," Fry said, as the two walked as fast as they could without drawing suspicion. "We've got two mobile units right behind her, and two out in front guessing which way she'll walk. She's in good hands."

"I'm not going to relax until I get her away from that thug. I swear to God, Fry, if he puts one hand on her . . ."

"I know, Chuck, I know. But like I said, she's a big girl and can apparently handle herself."

Several minutes later, Jana and Jeffrey Dima turned on W. Twenty-Sixth Street.

"Shit," Stone said, "they turned. The two mobile units walking out in front of her are now out of position."

"Would you calm down?" Agent Fry said as he put a hand on Stone's shoulder. "You know as well as I do that that's what happens. Any surveillance units out in front will generally get out of position at one time or another because they can't predict which way the subject is going to go." Fry pushed against a hidden ear piece and spoke into the mic tucked inside his shirt collar.

"Mobile one and three, you're out of the lane. Subjects now headed west on Twenty-Sixth. Hightail it through Madison Square Park until you come out at the intersection of Fifth Avenue at Twenty-Sixth. If you hurry, you'll be just ahead of them."

The two young surveillance specialists, one a male, the other a female, broke into a sprint, weaving in between people on the sidewalk, then turned into the park to try to run ahead of Jana.

The radio cracked to life. "Six, six? This is mobile four. We've lost visual! I repeat, we've lost visual."

22

Decrypting the Data

"Well find them, dammit!" Stone barked into the radio. He broke into a run doing his best to weave in and out of people on the sidewalk in front of him, but then remembered that Jana was wearing the tiny tracker device. As long as she was outdoors, he could find her location. He pulled out his phone and opened the app. "We're okay. I show her taking a left on Fifth. They're headed right where they said they were, to Jeffrey Dima's building. We need to put eyes on them immediately. And when you reacquire, don't lose sight of them again."

"Yes, sir," came the reply from one of the mobile surveillance specialists as he panted, trying to catch his breath. A few moments later, the specialist said, "Six, six, this is mobile three. We've got her in visual. Heading down Fifth. Hold on, six . . . looks like, yes, looks like they're entering a nightclub. The Forty-Forty Club. It's an upscale place at the bottom of the 10 Madison Square West building."

"Roger that, mobile three. Don't make it obvious, but get in that club and observe. I don't want her alone with that thug unless we can see what's going on."

"Ah, sir?" mobile three replied, "that might be kind of a problem."

"And why is that?"

"That's an exclusive club, sir. Members only. I'll never get inside there without drawing attention."

"Shit," Stone said to Agent Fry. "I don't want her alone."

"Stone," Fry said, "this is part of the deal. She's already committed to going to the guy's penthouse, where she knows we can't listen in. This nightclub isn't as dangerous as when she goes upstairs. It might be a members-only club, but it's a public place. He isn't going to harm her in there."

"I hear you, but dammit, if anything happens to that girl . . ."

"Jesus, to listen to you, you'd think it was your daughter we're talking about."

Stone picked up his pace again. "My daughter? *My* daughter? No shit, Fry. I guess you didn't notice what Jana's birth date was. What am I talking about? You wouldn't know the significance anyway."

"Her birth date? What about it?"

"October nineteenth, 1986," Stone replied as he sidestepped a woman pulling a rolling suitcase up the sidewalk.

"What's October nineteenth?"

Stone paused a few moments. "It's my daughter's birthday, to the exact day and year."

Fry's gaze trailed off into the distance. "Your daughter . . . I didn't know you had kids."

"My son is twenty-four now. My Jennifer . . . we called her Jenna, was born on October nineteenth, 1986, same day as Jana Baker," Stone swallowed a lump in his throat. "She was a preemie, though. Only one and a half pounds. She was a fighter. Toughest little thing I ever saw. She was only with us nine months before . . ."

"God, I'm sorry," Fry said. "You never told me. Listen, Stone, I

86

know you've gotten close to Jana. But look at me, she's going to be all right."

"Thanks, man, but I don't think I could ever forgive myself if anything happens to her."

"There are twelve of us on-site here. That's a lot of guns. We're going to do everything we can to keep her safe."

"Mobile two, three, four, and five are all in position," barked Stone's radio.

"Roger that," Stone said into the mic. "I don't care that we can't laser-mic the penthouse. I want two sets of eyes in the building across the street. We still might be able to see through the glass."

"This is mobile two. Roger that, sir. And, sir? I'm familiar with Jeffrey Dima's building. Be advised, the subjects won't have to exit the club if they intend on going up to the penthouse. The club is enormous. It takes up much of the first floor of this building. There's an entrance from inside the building lobby to the club, and an elevator right there."

Stone again spoke into the mic. "Mobile two, you seem awfully familiar with the layout of this building."

"Been here before, sir. Back when we were assigned to surveil the CEO, Rune Dima. He lives here too."

"Both cousins live in the same building? How convenient," Stone said to Fry.

Fry replied, "Right. Rune is a floor below Jeffrey. Sorry, never mentioned the fact that they live in the same place."

"Doesn't matter," Stone said. "But it is kind of odd, isn't it? I mean, the fact that the CEO of the company lives in a less expensive place than the CFO." Then into his mic, he said, "Roger that, mobile two. Rune Dima is not our target. You just focus on Jeffrey. And put a unit inside the lobby. Tell him to talk his way past the doorman. I want to know when the subjects hit that elevator." Stone lowered the mic then closed his eyes and thought about his next tactical decision. "Fry, is our Enhanced Special Weapons and Tactics team in position?"

"It's not an enhanced unit, just the standard SWAT team out of the Manhattan field office. But yes, they're in place. We've got them split into two minivans, parked on opposite corners of Madison Square Park right now."

"Why the hell didn't they send the enhanced unit? Dammit, I specifically said I wanted Enhanced SWAT."

"Don't shoot the messenger. You know as well as I do that there are only nine enhanced units in the bureau, and one of them is deployed overseas at the moment. The director holds them and all hostage rescue teams in reserve for counter-terrorism operations, and you know it."

"And what the hell does he call this? Rune and Jeffrey Dima are known terrorists."

"Other than the communiqués with Al-Jawary, and the obvious fact that they're almost certainly in possession of insider trading information, we have nothing on them. If the director thought they were about to attack the United States, he'd send us one of the enhanced teams, a team from FBI Hostage Rescue, a couple of Navy SEALs, and even my mother-in-law. But as it stands, we have squat to offer him."

"All right, all right. I just expected more firepower, that's all." Stone smirked. "Your mother-in-law? She's a piece of work, huh?"

"Don't get me started," Agent Fry replied.

"So wait, the SWAT team is sitting in a couple of minivans?"

"Yeah, you wanted us to blend in and not be seen, remember?"

Stone looked through a compact set of binoculars toward the entrance to The 40/40 Club. "So where did we get ahold of minivans? We don't have anything like that in the motor pool."

"To be honest, I only know where one of them came from."

"Which was?" Stone said, still focusing through the binoculars.

"It's that guy the director talks to at NSA. It's his wife's."

"Bill Tarleton? You're telling me that the guy known as Uncle Bill lent his wife's minivan to us for this operation? Boy, the director is really calling in favors."

"Oh, it gets better. Uncle Bill is apparently *driving* it himself. He's here, parked just behind the building."

"He's *here?*" Stone pulled the binoculars away from his face and looked at Fry. "He's a directory head, or a section chief, or some other such thing at the National Security Agency. What the hell is he doing here with my SWAT team?"

"Remember, he and FBI Director Latent were roommates at Georgetown. They've known each other for years. And something else—Bill Tarleton has apparently been chewing Latent's ear off about what he believes to be a pending attack. Uncle Bill insisted on being on-site here to decrypt the data as soon as Miss Baker gets her hands on it."

"How is it that I wasn't told about this?"

"You assigned me to relay info back and forth with Director Latent to keep him up to speed on the case. Guess it slipped my mind, Boss. Sorry."

Stone put the binoculars back to his face and again focused on the entrance to the club. "Slipped your mind? Hmmm, I wonder what might have slipped *my* mind recently. What was it that crossed my desk last week? Let me think. Oh yeah, that request you put in for transfer to the bureau's Hazardous Material Response Unit. You know, I would approve it for you, but it *slipped my mind.*"

"Very funny, Boss. Very funny."

23

Elevator to the Unknown

Inside The 40/40 Club, Jana watched the bartender like a hawk. She was mostly concerned with keeping tabs on Jeffrey to ensure he did not slip a powdered Rohypnol into her wine glass, but it occurred to her that she should be wary of the bartender as well. After all, if he was working for Jeffrey, Jana could end up drugged and sexually assaulted before she even knew what had happened. No, her goal was vigilance—she would not be a victim. In fact, she had every intention of finding evidence that would lead the FBI to whatever the Dima terrorists had planned. She placed a tiny strip of the test paper between her fingers, and dipped it into the wine just as Jeffrey nodded to the bartender. The paper came back blank.

For some reason, Jana felt more alive than she could ever remember. Her life up to this moment had been one of such predictability. But now, in the most dangerous situation she had ever imagined, her pulse raced. It was an exhilaration she had not counted on.

Adrenaline pulsed as her goal came front and center in her mind. *The data, I must get the data. I am the only one who can stop them.* She smiled at Jeffrey, allowing herself to go deeper into the undercover role. To Jana, the acting was also exciting. She'd never role-played before, and now that it was happening with the stakes so high, she wondered why she'd never thought of a career in law enforcement before.

Jeffrey grinned and his pearly white teeth gleamed back at Jana.

He's not a bad-looking guy, Jana thought. A slimeball, certainly, but in different circumstances, she wondered if she'd have been attracted to him. Jana allowed her eyes to wander to Jeffrey's chest as he shed his business jacket and loosened his two-hundred-dollar Armani tie. Her gaze did not go unnoticed.

"There's something different about you," Jeffrey said. "I don't know what it is."

"Is that your best line?" Jana giggled as she tapped the top of his thigh. "Does that work on the other ladies?"

"You're a tough one, aren't you?"

"I'm just messing with you," she said. "Something different about me? Are you sure it's just that you haven't ever slept with me, so that's what's different?"

"Ouch," Jeffrey laughed. "I'm not that bad."

"That's not what I hear. I hear you're a bad boy." Her coyness was disarming.

"You think I'm a bad boy, do you? But you're still here."

"Maybe I like bad boys."

"You don't strike me as the kind of girl that likes bad boys."

I do not like bad boys, Jana thought. *Keep stringing him along.*

Jana took a sip of wine. "And yet here I am."

"Yes, here you are." Jeffrey ran his eyes across her figure again. "And I'm glad you are, Miss Baker. You're a beautiful woman."

"Would you call me Jana, already?" She took another sip of wine but noticed the slight shaking of her hand and the sight startled her.

***

"Tell me again why she wanted to go for a drink with him before going to his apartment," Agent Fry said to Stone as the two took up position in a cafe across the street.

"She didn't want to give him a chance to get back to his penthouse first. She wanted to keep an eye on him so he didn't have time to set anything up, like adding a dose of Rohypnol into a glass without her knowing."

"And she's got the paper test strips? The ones that detect the drug?"

"Yeah, I gave them to her this morning. Every young woman in America should have those things. She knows to not put anything in her mouth without secretly touching a test strip to it first."

"And you're sure she can pull off her plan once she's inside?"

"Hell no I'm not sure," Stone barked. "I'm scared. *She's* the one who's so damn sure."

"You're grumpy," Fry said. "You didn't sleep last night, did you?"

"How was I supposed to sleep with this about to go down? It didn't help that Uncle Bill at NSA calls me at all hours of the night."

***

About an hour later, Jeffrey stood from the plush leather-covered barstool. "You getting hungry? I'm a hell of a cook."

Yeah, I bet you are, Jana thought. "Starved," she said. "Is this how you get all the women? You're a gourmet cook?"

"You know what they say."

"The way to a woman's heart is through her stomach." She glanced Jeffrey up and down then said, "But I doubt it's my heart you're after."

"You're bad," Jeffrey said as he put his arm around her and walked toward the lobby.

***

A whispered call came across the radio. "Six, six, this is mobile two. Subjects just came into the lobby. Heading onto the elevator now."

"Here we go," Stone said as he passed a hand across his balding forehead. "Roger that, mobile two," he said into the radio. He turned to Agent Fry. "Heading up the elevator. Dammit, this is going to kill me, this blindness." He raised the radio again. "Mobile one? From your vantage point across the street, you have the best view. You are our eyes now. I want you to call out anything you can see in that penthouse."

"Roger that, six," came the chirped reply.

Agent Fry put a hand on Stone's shoulder to calm him. "All units, all units," he said into the radio. "Be on full alert. We could call at any moment to raid the penthouse."

The leaders from each SWAT team replied in turn.

"Relax, Stone. We've got her covered. She's going to be okay."

"That's what I keep telling myself," Stone said, but then shook his head. "I've got to be closer to this thing. I'm going across the street. I'll talk my way past the doorman and get upstairs, somewhere."

24

In the Penthouse

I've got to find his stash of roofies, Jana thought.

"My, my, Jeffrey. You certainly have decorated well."

The sprawling penthouse was an open floor plan, decorated in young, New York style. Walls of glass spanned the entire expanse—the view of Manhattan was stunning.

"I can't take credit for it," Jeffrey said as he walked toward the built-in Sub-Zero refrigerator. "I cheated and hired a decorator."

Jana watched him. *Unless he took a capsule of Rohypnol to work with him this morning, he doesn't have any on his person. Most likely place he'd keep them is in his bathroom.*

***

"Six, this is mobile two. Subjects are inside the apartment."

"Roger that, mobile two. Keep your optics trained on the suspect. If you see him dump anything into her drink or food, you call it out."

"Roger that, six."

***

"Can I use the ladies room?" Jana said with a little grin.

"Just down the hall on the left."

Jana walked down the carpeted hallway but when she found the bathroom she realized it was a guest bath, not the one Jeffrey would normally use. She looked back toward the main living area to make sure he couldn't see her, then tiptoed until she entered what was certainly Jeffrey's master bedroom. The bed was massive and sat low to the ground, a black leather-covered comforter lay across it.

Leather? A leather comforter? What a prick, she thought. She walked further around to the left until she found his master bath, a sprawling collaboration of black marble and mirrors. She started to walk in but feared her heels would clack against the marble floor, so she removed them. She walked in and began pulling open drawers in a frantic attempt to locate Jeffrey's supply of Rohypnol before he could use it on her. If she could locate his supply, her plan stood a good chance of working. But even when she opened the medicine cabinet, she could see nothing out of the ordinary. Just typical over-the-counter items, toilet paper, and extra towels. *Where the hell is it? How am I going to find it? I've got to think like him. Where would he put it? Where would a raping thug put his stash of roofies?* But then she saw the door to his walk-in closet and a thought struck her. *His closet. What about his closet? Maybe it's in there.* She looked over her shoulder again and walked in. *If he catches me in here . . .*

***

"Six, this is mobile two. I've lost her. I don't have eyes on her anymore."

"Dammit!" Stone barked into the radio from his new position in the building, a stairwell on the opposite end, just two floors below the penthouse.

"I've got Dima in play, but she walked down a hallway. Hold on, six. Hold on . . . he's walking down the hallway in her direction!"

"I've had enough of this!" Stone said. "I'm going in."

"No, wait," Agent Fry called across the radio. "He hasn't had time to drug her. She's not in danger yet. And remember, we have no evidence against him."

"We've got him in communication with a known terrorist network."

"If you go in there before we have the evidence, it'll never stick. And, they'll cancel whatever terror attack they've got planned and do it later, without our knowing. We've got to give her more time."

A vein in Stone's temple pulsed. He paused, but finally raised the radio and spoke into the mic. "I hate it when you're right."

***

In the middle of the closet sat a center island filled with drawers. But what astounded Jana was the number of business suits, casual slacks, and dress shirts. Each was hung on a long rack that ran the circumference of the room, separated by the exact same amount of space. The man was a perfectionist, and a real clothes hog. *These must be two-thousand-dollar suits,* she thought. *Look at all those shoes. There's got to be one hundred and fifty thousand dollars of clothes in here. What a jackass.* She began opening drawer after drawer on the center island only to find perfectly folded socks in one, unopened dress shirts in another, and an electric shoe polisher in a third. *Where the hell is it?* She began to perspire as the pressure of finding the drugs before she got caught increased.

It was then she saw a single dress shirt hanging on the wall with a pair of slacks, right next to the full-length mirror. They had been separated from all the other clothing. It was as if he had set these items aside to put on later. She quickstepped to the full-length mirror and felt the pocket on the dress shirt but found it empty. When she felt a lump in the pants pocket, however, her hand darted inside it. Her fingers landed on a tiny Ziploc baggie that contained two capsules. *Found them, you asshole.* Upon closer examination, Jana could see that the capsules were an exact match to the ones Agent Stone had given her. Each capsule was blue and white, imprinted with the words *Flunitrazepam, 1 mg, Roche.*

She fished in her handbag and withdrew two identical capsules from her prescription bottle and carefully replaced them with the two from Jeffrey's pant pocket. Jana had previously emptied the powdered contents of her Rohypnol and replaced it with confectioner's sugar. If Jeffrey tried to drug her, nothing would happen; she would simply detect the sweet taste of sugar.

"What are you doing in here?" Jeffrey's voice said from behind. Jana's pulse rate exploded.

25

Making the Switch

The minutes ticked by. Stone wiped the blush of sweat from his upper lip. "Mobile two, give me an update. What's going on up there?"

"Six, this is mobile two. I've got nothing. They haven't come back into view. I'm blind."

"I can't take this anymore," Stone said as he began to stand up.

***

Oh my god, he saw me. "Uh, I guess you're wondering what I'm doing in your closet. Well, I just . . ." *Think, dammit, think.* "I just wanted to see it, that's all. Um, I kind of have a problem with that, you know?"

Jeffrey scowled at her while Jana's hand trembled behind her back. "What kind of a problem?" he said.

"I kind of have a thing for well-dressed men. I like to see the clothes a guy has. Kind of a sickness, I guess. It's just that . . . I can tell a lot about a man by the way he dresses, that's all."

"Oh. Well that's not so bad. Why didn't you just ask me?"

"I didn't want to be so forward." Jana felt a drop of perspiration roll from under her right arm and drip against the side of her tight shirt.

Jeffrey's smile returned. "And I wasn't checking on you. I was just coming back here to change out of these work clothes."

"I'll just wait out there on the couch."

"You sure you don't want to stay while I change?" he said as his grin again exposed his teeth.

"I'm not *that* easy," she said as she breezed past him and let her fingers run across his chest.

***

"Hold on, six," the radio barked. "I've got her now. She's come back to the living area."

Stone breathed a sigh of relief. He had almost run up the two flights of stairs on his way to pull Jana out, investigation be damned. "Roger that, mobile two," he said, wiping sweat from his forehead. "What's happening now? Do you see Dima?"

"Negative, six. The subject is not in play. She just walked into the kitchen though. She's looking down the hallway and pulling something from her purse. What the hell is she doing?"

There was a protracted silence.

Stone could wait no longer. "Don't make me come up there and thump your skull," Stone said into the radio. "What do you see?"

"She's pulling the cork out of a bottle of wine."

Stone said, "Here she goes. She's going to do it now. Damn that girl has guts."

"She just poured two glasses of wine . . . and . . . shit, she just emptied a capsule of powder into one of them. What the hell is going on?"

"Mobile two, this is six," Agent Stone said. "All part of the plan. Is Dima in sight?"

"Negative, six. She's still looking down the hallway. She's stirring the powdered substance into the wine now. Is she drugging him or something?"

***

Jana separated the capsule and dumped a full dose of Rohypnol into the wine glass she intended for Dima to drink. Her heart felt like it might leap from her chest and she tried to steady her hand. *I've got to calm down or he's going to see my hand shaking.* She placed the drugged wine glass on the top of the counter and took her own to the couch. She sat down, slipped her heels off, and pulled her legs up to curl them beneath her. *Does this look enticing enough?* she wondered. *Calm down, just calm down.* She drew in three deep breaths and blew them out in tandem. *He's got to believe you are here for him. You can't let him suspect anything or the investigation will be blown.* She took a sip of wine then glanced down at her blouse. With the flick of a finger she unbuttoned the top two buttons to expose just enough of her chest to look enticing, but not slutty.

Jeffrey emerged from the back, wearing the clothes that were hanging by the full-length mirror. Jana looked him up and down.

"Very nice," she said.

"I was hoping you would like it."

"I poured us some wine. I hope you don't mind."

He walked into the kitchen but stopped abruptly at the counter, then picked up the bottle. The label read: 2009 Opus One. Cabernet, California.

"My, my," he said. "You do have good taste in wine. This is a seven-hundred-dollar bottle."

"Oh, crap," Jana said as she held a hand to her mouth. "I'm sorry."

"No, it's fine. Was looking forward to drinking this." Jeffrey grabbed his wine glass, took a sip and smiled. He walked to the couch and sat next to her. "The wine's incredible, isn't it? So whatever are we to talk about?"

"Whatever comes to mind. Like you, where are you from?"

"Me? Oh that's boring. My parents were from Syria but I grew up here."

"You know," Jana said, "this might be the best wine I've ever had."

Jeffrey took another sip and let his eyes roll down to the lowest point of exposed skin on her chest.

***

"They're on the couch together," mobile one said. "Glass of wine in hand."

"Is he thirsty?" Stone said into the mic.

"Roger that, six. He's drinking his."

"And what's Jana doing?" Stone said. He was in a struggle to vacuum up enough information to know whether she was safe or not.

"Well, she's having some wine too. And from the looks of it, I'd say she's trying to . . ."

"Trying to what?"

"Trying to seduce him," mobile one said. "She unbuttoned a couple of buttons on her blouse. Sorry, sir. It's just that she's either interested in the guy, or putting on a pretty powerful act."

Stone thought to himself, *This is unlike any witness I've ever worked with. She's a natural.*

Mobile one said, "Is this part of the plan? To seduce the guy?"

"No, nimrod. She's trying to play along on the date so he thinks she's interested. We're trying to avoid him becoming suspicious of why she's there."

***

Jeffrey took a large sip and slid closer to Jana.

She put a hand on his chest to slow his advance. "Hold on there, smooth talker. I'm not that drunk."

"Well, maybe we should get you there then." Jeffrey tilted Jana's wine glass to her mouth as she finished the last of it.

"That wine . . ."

"Yeah, I know," Jeffrey said. "An incredible thing, isn't it?"

"And what about you?" Jana said, nodding to Jeffrey's wine glass.

He tilted it to his mouth until it was empty. He then stood and took both glasses to the kitchen and placed them in front of the bottle and began to fish in his pant pocket.

***

"Six? This is mobile one. He's refilling their glasses. Hold on, he's got something in his hand. He just dumped something in her drink!"

"Now's when I get really nervous," Stone said to himself. "Roger that, mobile one. If she was able to make the switch, that's part of the plan too."

Fry said into his mic. "And if she wasn't able to make the switch?"

"She will test the wine before she drinks it to make sure. I was adamant about that with her."

***

Jana pulled out another tiny sliver of thin, white paper from its hiding place underneath her wrist watch and palmed it. When Jeffrey handed the freshly refilled wine glass to her, she dropped it in and watched to ensure it did not turn bright pink in color, a telltale detection of Rohypnol. When the paper did not turn, she took a full gulp of wine, being sure to swallow the square of paper in the process. The taste was much sweeter than the last glass and Jana knew, he had tried to drug her.

"You *are* thirsty, aren't you?" Jeffrey laughed as he flopped onto the couch. Jana could not help but notice his eyes had already started to become glassy. "Drink up," he said.

She complied and smiled at him. "I like hanging out with you," she said as she put her hand on his leg.

He looked at the hand and glanced at her with bedroom eyes, then slid closer.

***

"He's making his move," mobile one said across the radio. "Yeah, he's kissing her neck. But he looks drunk or something."

"Thank God," Stone said. "She got the drugs into him. He better not put an unwanted hand on her—"

"This was all *her* plan? To make out with the guy?" Agent Fry said. "She thought this whole thing up? You're right, she's got guts."

"What's happening now?" Stone said into the mic.

"Well, he kind of leaned his weight onto her, but more like he's drunk than anything else. And, he's ah . . . uh oh. He's unbuttoning her blouse."

"He's what?" Stone blurted into the radio. "Is she okay? Does she look panicked?"

"Negative, sir. She doesn't look scared at all."

"I can't believe she's letting him do this," Fry said.

"Don't get me started," Stone replied. "Keep up the description of what's happening, mobile one."

"She's finished with her wine, and he's still working the blouse. Having a little trouble with the buttons."

"The drugs are working on him," Stone said. "Serves the prick right, trying to drug a woman like that."

Mobile one continued. "Wait a second, she just stood up. She's *unbuttoning* her blouse. Oh, yeah, it's dropped to the floor now, sir. She's down to her bra. Is it okay for us to be watching this?"

Stone buried his face in his hands. "Oh my God. I can't believe I talked her into being a material witness. I'm going to burn in hell for this."

Agent Fry said, "You didn't tell her to take her damn clothes off!" Fry said into the radio. "Just keep watching and relaying information, mobile one."

"He looks like he's out," mobile one said. "He just slumped over on the couch. Now she's running toward the back rooms. She left her blouse on the floor."

***

Jana could think of nothing other than searching the apartment to find whatever evidence there might be. *It would be a laptop,* she thought. *Whatever we find, it's got to be on a laptop, if I could only find the thing.* She ran into the bedroom and opened one drawer after another. "A laptop, a laptop. Where would he put his laptop?" But it wasn't until she looked under the bed that she spotted it. She ran it back into the living area, looked over at Jeffrey, and sat at the dining table in full view of the massive span of windows. "Just making sure you don't wake up, you prick," she said out loud, then jumped up to grab her purse. She pulled her phone from it and dialed Agent Stone.

He answered and Jana could hear the rapidity of his breathing.

"Jana? You all right?"

"Fine. I assume you're watching. I've got his laptop. It's booting up now."

"Yes, we're watching. Do you want to explain to me where your blouse is right now?"

Jana glanced down at her bra. "Oh, shit. Well, Dad, kind of had to improvise there. He wasn't passing out fast enough. Had to make it look authentic."

"Authentic? My surveillance team in the office across the street are males. They thought they were watching a peep show."

"Can we stay on point here?" Jana said with a steeliness in her voice.

"Man, who's the federal agent?" Stone laughed. "All right, what's the laptop doing?"

"Crap, it's looking for a password. I'll never find his password. Stone, can you hack it?"

"Not in the thirty minutes we have before he wakes up, no."

"Wait a minute," she said. "The laptop has a fingerprint scanner on it." She glanced over at Jeffrey. "I know exactly what to do."

***

"Six, this is mobile one. She's walked over to the subject with the laptop and she's kneeling down. What's she doing? Wait, looks like she's swiping his finger across the face of the laptop. I'll be damned."

***

"Good thinking, Jana," Stone said. His voice mottled with pride.

"Okay, I'm in. I have no idea what I'm looking for though, so I'm going to copy the entire hard disk onto the thumb drive you gave me. "

"Exactly. Then get the hell out of there, Jana. We've got NSA on standby to examine and, if needed, decrypt the files."

"All right," Jana said.

To Stone, Jana's voice sounded like cold granite.

She continued. "It's copying now. Are we sure this flash drive is big enough to hold an entire hard drive?"

"Plenty," Stone replied. "And Jana, while it copies, you might want to put your clothes back on."

"Right," she said through a slight grin.

"Once it finishes copying, put the laptop back where you found it. I want you out of that apartment and down in the lobby with the data as fast as possible. When Jeffrey wakes up, he won't even know what happened, much less that we copied all the contents of his computer."

But then she heard the sound of a key being pushed into the lock on the front door and she froze. Her eyes widened as the door handle turned.

26

Enter the Demon

"Oh, Christ," came a whispered transmission across the radio, but then mobile one's volume escalated, "Six, we've got a problem! Someone just entered through the front door! Male, dark complected . . . he's got a weapon!"

***

Jana's mouth dropped open as Rune Dima walked into the apartment, a Glock in his hand. The look of surprise on his face was paralleled by her own.

"What are you doing here?" Rune barked, the look of shock still painted on him.

"I'm, I'm, ah, well . . ." Jana picked up the laptop and held it over her bra. "I just had some more work to do and thought—"

"You had some work to do?" Rune said as he walked toward Jana, his gun pointed forward. "And you thought you'd come over to Jeffrey's penthouse and what? Collaborate with him?" His eyes wandered down Jana's body. "And I suppose his air conditioning was out and you got hot? Figured you'd be more comfortable if you worked with your top off? Is that it?"

Go ahead, she thought, *talk your way out of that one*. Jana looked down at her bra and continued backpedaling toward the couch and sliding glass door that led onto the balcony. She glanced at the laptop screen where the files were still being copied. The open window on the monitor read *65% complete.*

"Mr. Dima—"

"Rune," he smiled, still walking toward her. "I told you to call me Rune."

Oh my God, he's going to kill me. "My blouse . . . Jeffrey and I—"

"Yes, you and Jeffrey have obviously become involved with one another. A liability I'm sad to say I cannot afford. Where is *Jeffrey,* anyway?" He spat the name like sour vinegar. But then Rune walked close enough to the couch to see that Jeffrey was slumped over on it, unconscious.

Jana's hand shook harder now. Her first thought was to lunge for her purse to pull out her handgun, but she knew she'd never get to it before being shot to death. She scrambled to come up with a story to stall him until the files had finished copying.

"Mr. Dima . . . Rune, Jeffrey and I were on a date. Yes, I admit that. And, and, we had some wine and I guess he had too much because he passed out." She was almost speed-talking as she continued to backpedal past the couch. "And you've been so good to me." She glanced at the laptop, *85% complete.* "I am just so sorry." She reached down and picked her blouse off the arm of the couch then used it to cover the USB flash drive which protruded from the side of the laptop. "I know I shouldn't have gotten involved with him."

Rune interrupted, "No, you should not have. But as it turns out, Miss Baker, your usefulness to this company has come to an end. I'm afraid you know too much."

"Oh, Mr. Dim . . . Rune, I don't know anything. I mean, what's there to know?" She backed into the sliding glass door of the balcony with a thud, then fumbled behind herself until she found the door handle. She slid the door open and her eyes cast a furtive glance to the laptop, *99% complete*. Her mind raced. *Keep him talking.*

***

"She's backed out onto the balcony!" mobile one yelled into the radio. "Jesus Christ! Why don't we have a sniper up here? He's going to kill her!"

***

"Do you think backing out onto this balcony is going to save you?" Rune said as he screwed a silencer onto the barrel of the Glock. "I'm afraid I must erase my tracks, Miss Baker." He glanced back at Jeffrey's unconscious body. "Both you and Jeffrey."

The instant Rune looked away, Jana yanked the thumb drive out, dropped the laptop onto a padded patio chair, then wrapped the thumb drive inside the blouse, and threw the bundle over the balcony.

***

Mobile one yelled into the radio, "She just threw her blouse over the balcony. It's drifting to the street. Why would she . . . wait a minute," he said as he squinted through binoculars at the side of the laptop in Jana's hands, "the thumb drive isn't in the laptop anymore. I think she just threw it over the side, wrapped in her blouse!"

***

Rune snapped his head at her. "What was that? Why did you just throw your blouse over the balcony?"

Jana knew the moment Rune Dima had entered the apartment the FBI operation to *secretly* steal the data was blown. She had the data but had been caught in the act. There was no point hiding that fact now.

"It's over, Rune," Jana said with a soft, feminine quality to her voice. It's all over now. They know everything. You don't need

109

to continue."

He stammered as his mind raced to comprehend why Jana had thrown her blouse over the balcony. "What's over?" But then his eyes landed on the laptop and he lunged for it. "This is *Jeffrey's* laptop, isn't it?" He was almost yelling. "What are you doing with Jeffrey's laptop?"

He jammed his hand onto her throat and crunched down. She flailed her hands until they landed on his forearm, an effort to stop him from choking her. He then pushed her against the balcony railing. Jana's body leaned backward, as her fingernails dug into the flesh of his forearm.

***

"He's about to throw her off the balcony!" mobile one screamed.

***

"Rune, no!" she gasped through his choking grip. But it was too late. He leaned his full weight forward and pushed her over the rounded metal railing.

She flopped over the side but did not abate her hold on his arm. Her body dangled forty-one stories above Fifth Avenue.

A gunshot from Agent Stone's .40 caliber Glock ruptured the air and he leapt onto the balcony. The bullet struck Rune in the rib cage and Stone lunged over the edge to grab Jana. Rune recoiled from the impact but raised his gun and shot Stone at point-blank range just as Jana's flailing right leg found the ledge. Stone fell back, clutching his chest, and collapsed. With her leg, Jana pushed against the balcony to raise herself, then wrapped her arms around Rune's neck and leapt onto him.

"No!" she screamed as she pushed into Rune to prevent him from shooting Stone again. Rune struggled but wrenched a forearm around her neck and yanked it tight, again choking her. He pointed the gun at Stone but Jana raised a knee into the air and slammed her heel into the dorsal lateral cutaneous nerve in his foot and Rune buckled to the ground. Jana fell back with him and began smashing the back of her head into Rune's nose. The forearm crushing her neck lost power and she pulled herself free and up onto her feet. She then jammed her heel into Rune's wrist in repeated succession until the Glock spun out of his grip. She grabbed the gun and pointed it at him, towering over the man. Her adrenaline was pulsing.

The front door of the apartment burst open and eight heavily armed and Kevlar-laden SWAT team members burst in.

"FBI! Everybody on the ground!" they yelled with weapons forward.

Jana heard the commotion but did not move. She could not pull her gaze off Rune Dima who lay beneath her. Blood spurted from the bullet hole in his chest and she pointed the gun at him.

"What are you going to do?" Rune said as he coughed out bright red blood. "Kill me? You're a woman. You don't have the guts. Besides, you can't stop the operation from going forward now. It's too late. Our plan is already in full swing."

Jana's clenched her teeth and the grip on the Glock tightened. "Don't test me, you son of a bitch." She applied tension to the trigger.

"Jana, no," Stone said from the ground as he pressed against his wound.

She glanced back at him with a strange look. To Stone, the look appeared to be a concoction of anger and death, mottled into the beauty of her eyes.

"Not like this, Jana. You don't want to do this."

But she turned her glare back to Rune.

Stone continued speaking through fits and gasps. "I've been there, Jana. I've stood where you're standing. He almost killed you. Adrenaline and fury raging through you. You don't want to live with this."

SWAT members registered the scene and eased onto the balcony, but Stone held up his hand to stop them.

"Look at me, Jana," Stone said, his voice that of a calm father. "You mean too much to me. I don't want to see you do anything you're going to regret for the rest of your life."

Jana eased off the trigger and looked at him. *My God*, she thought. *What am I doing?*

"My grandpa used to say that to me." A tear eased its way into her vision as the adrenaline rush began to take its toll. "He used to tell me that all the time. Never do anything you're going to regret for the rest of your life."

One of the SWAT team members rushed forward and took the gun from her, then searched Rune for other weapons. One of the men began applying pressure to Rune's chest in an effort to stop the bleeding. Jana knelt down to Agent Stone and did the same.

***

On the street below, the second minivan, this one driven by Uncle Bill Tarleton, raced forward and screeched its tires next to the blouse. Bill jumped out of the van and grabbed it, then unfolded it until the thumb drive fell out. "Damn that kid's good," he said as he jumped in the back of the van and placed the drive into a USB port on the side of his laptop. "Now, let's take a look at this thumb drive and see what these assholes have been hiding."

***

Jana applied pressure to Stone's chest but blood continued to ease out around her fingers.

"Medic!" she yelled. "We need two medics up here!"

"Way ahead of you, ma'am," one of the SWAT members said as he checked Stone's pulse. "We've got a helicopter evac en route.

ETA one minute."

"You hear that, Stone?" Jana said through a false smile. "Help's on the way."

"Listen, Jana," Stone said. "I don't want you to worry about me." His eyes closed but he continued talking. "You did good, kid. You did really, really good. I'm so proud of you." He seemed to drift off.

"Hey," she said, "stay with me, okay? Keep looking me in the eyes." A tear rolled off her cheek and plopped on the back of her hand. It mixed with Stone's fresh blood into a murky swirl.

"We're losing him!" the SWAT member said into the mic. "Where's my chopper?"

Jana shook Stone and his eyes flickered.

"Whatever happens," he whispered. "You're going to be fine. Your life is going to be just fine." His eyes closed again.

"Stone? Stone?" she said as she shook him. "Don't you leave me!"

27

The Funeral

The cemetery in Brooklyn, New York, was strangely beautiful in Jana's eyes. It was bordered by three other cemeteries, all blending together into one, the combined greenery stretching across hundreds of tree-lined acres. It had been two months since the series of events that led her here. Jana stood far back from the small group of mourners as they gathered around the grave site. She felt like an outsider, a person whose presence might not be wanted in the midst of grieving friends and relatives. Standing beneath a large oak tree, she glanced up at brilliant yellow-green light glowing through the leaves, then to the slivers of blue sky intermixed between them.

She heard the quiet sound of footsteps on the ground behind her and she turned.

"Hello, young lady," Agent Stone said with a grin.

"I thought I might see you here," she said. "Hey, you look like shit."

"Thank you."

"You look a hell of a lot better than you did on that balcony though. I really thought I'd lost you."

"You and me both," he said, then walked up and put his arm around her shoulder. "I'm a little surprised you are here though."

"So am I," she said as her gaze returned to the circle of mourners listening to the burial service. "I didn't think I'd come." Then her head shook. "I don't know why I'm here."

"You lived through a lot, Jana. What you went through wouldn't be easy for anyone to handle."

She smirked at him. "What I went through? *You* got shot."

"That's right. I did, didn't I? I almost forgot."

"Very funny. Well, no, it's not funny, actually." Jana shook her head. "Your job . . . I can't decide whether it's the most noble thing I've ever heard of, or the craziest."

"A little of both, I think," he said through a laugh.

"Agent Fry told me you have an adult son. He also told me about your daughter," Jana said to him. "He said she died when she was just nine months old? I know it was a long time ago, but I'm really sorry you lost her."

Stone swallowed.

"He also said she and I share the same birthday. Is that true?"

"Yes."

"My God, I'm exactly the same age, down to the day? I think I'm starting to understand why you looked out for me so much."

"Yeah, well when I saw your birthdate, it brought back all those feelings."

"I can't imagine what that must have been like for you and your wife to go through."

"It's what eventually drove us apart," Stone said through a long exhale. "It was just too much. We were both just so hollowed out." He looked at the funeral service in the distance, and Jana could see the mist forming in his eyes. "My son's just a little older than you. He lived with his mom until he was old enough." Stone exhaled. "I hate cemeteries. I never used to though. I used to think it was so fascinating to walk through an old cemetery and look at the headstones. That probably sounds crazy, doesn't it?"

"Not crazy at all."

"My friends thought I was obsessed with death or something. But it was just the opposite. I was fascinated with *life*, with how these people lived. You see a lot of interesting things on an old headstone. The hand-carved lettering, the fonts and choice of words, the names and how long they lived. Anyway, the morning they lowered that tiny little casket into the ground with my little girl in it . . ." Stone stopped.

"You don't have to tell me if you don't want to," Jana said.

"Anyway, I've never wanted to look at headstones since."

A long silence ensued as they watched the service continue.

"Jeffrey Dima's arraignment is tomorrow," Stone said. "Thanks to you, the attack was stopped before it could wreak havoc on the global oil market."

He turned and looked across the grassy expanse at an FBI surveillance van parked in the distance. The van had been positioned in just such a way as to provide the best vantage point to photograph the funeral's attendees through high-powered optics. The photographs would later be scanned using facial-recognition software in an attempt to identify any other potential members of the terror cell.

"So this was all about oil," Jana said, a look of blankness in her eyes.

"The virus they embedded into their software would have given them complete control over every oil-drilling rig and pumping station in the Middle East. Every one that was owned by American interests, that is. But it was bigger than that. They not only would have been able to shut down oil production by controlling the software, but they would have also inflicted catastrophic physical damage to the facilities by shutting down valves and then pushing massive oil pressure onto them. A few hundred oil facilities would have been taken offline."

"I guess what we did was important."

"Important? Jana, in week one, gasoline would have gone to eight dollars per gallon, possibly over twelve dollars per gallon after that. It would have buckled the American economy."

"And from their investments, the Dima boys, along with Al-Qaeda, would have profited, and I helped them do it. I bought all those oil futures contracts for them. That's the insider trading the SEC could never pinpoint. The terrorists knew the oil market would skyrocket after they disrupted production, but no one knew how they knew."

"That's right. And what do you think Al-Qaeda would have done with several billion dollars in freshly acquired assets? They would have used that money to launch terror strikes against us. It would have funded any and every operation Osama bin Laden ever dreamed of. Do you realize with that kind of money, they could literally buy a nuclear warhead?"

"Who would sell them a warhead?"

"Don't be naive. When the USSR broke apart, do you think all their nukes were accounted for? Hell no. A few of those things made it onto the open market. Believe me, a billion dollars can buy just about anything."

They watched as the funeral continued.

"I'm going to have to testify at trial, aren't I?" Jana said.

Stone didn't answer.

She continued. "Go into open court and testify against Jeffrey Dima and the Al-Qaeda terror network." She shook her head. "I feel like I'm going to live the rest of my life looking over my shoulder."

"It's up to you, Jana. What you do or don't do, it's all up to you.

It's your life."

"Another flower delivery showed up at my doorstep."

"Let me guess," Stone said, "a single white rose?"

"Yes. A white rose is most often thought of as symbolizing new beginnings. But it can also symbolize *I'm thinking of you.*"

"Jeffrey Dima's sending you a message. Even while he's in prison, he wants to intimidate you, let you know he knows where you live, and he can get to you. Jana, even without your testimony, he's never going to see the light of day again."

They both looked toward the funeral service and watched as a casket containing the body of Rune Dima was lowered into the ground.

Jana nodded toward the service. "Stone?" she said through a tight throat. "I don't know how I'm supposed to feel about this."

"Hey, look at me. You aren't supposed to feel anything about the death of Rune Dima. You're just supposed to get on with your life. You owe the Dima cousins nothing."

"Is it that simple?" she said.

"Your old boss is being laid to rest right over there. You spent months working side by side with him. It turned out he was a bad guy, that's all. It will take time to wrap your head around it. But you'll figure it out."

"He seemed like such a good guy. He always treated me so well. I really thought Jeffrey was the one in charge, and not Rune. Jeffrey was always calling the shots, it seemed. But I guess I was wrong. Rune intended to kill both me and Jeffrey. I just don't know how I'm supposed to *trust* anymore. . ." Jana's voice trailed off. "What am I supposed to do now? Where am I supposed to go?"

"You're a young woman. You have your whole life in front of you. But I think you and I both know what path your life is supposed to take."

"I know," she whispered. "I know."

28

One Week Later

Avon Street Apartments, Queens, New York.

"Mrs. Merlinsky," Jana said, "I know I'm breaking my lease early. And I know that means I'm supposed to lose my first and last month's rent deposit. But please understand, if I stay here, they'll come for me."

"I don't understand," the old woman replied in a thick Polish accent.

"I was working for the FBI, Mrs. Merlinsky. I'm going to testify against a bunch of felons in federal court, and they want me dead. It's not safe for me here."

"That is not my problem," she said as her head tilted high into the air.

Jana's shoulders slumped. "Mrs. Merlinsky, do you have a family?"

"Of course I do," the woman said, a certain pride in her voice. "A daughter."

"And if your daughter got into trouble, through no fault of her own, and she was in danger from bad men, wouldn't you want her to get as far away from that place as possible?"

"Yes, but . . ."

Jana held the woman's hands. "Please, Mrs. Merlinsky."

The woman paused, but then nodded her head. "Of course I would, dear."

"Oh, thank you. Thank you."

"I'll return your rent deposit. You get far away from here, dear. And good luck to you."

Jana closed the apartment door behind her and stared at all the sealed cardboard boxes piled against the kitchen wall. She shook her head at the sight. "All my worldly possessions," she laughed. "Here it is, my life in a box." She looked around at the tiny studio apartment. "I never did wipe the protective layer of dust from the tops of those kitchen cabinets."

She picked up the first few boxes and loaded them onto a hand truck, then wheeled them out to the Silver Honda Odyssey minivan double-parked on the street out front. *It might be tight, but the boxes should all fit,* she thought. When the van was finally loaded, she went back inside and took one last look at the apartment, then got in the van and headed up Avon Street to Grand Central Parkway. She hopped on 495 past the Flushing Meadows National Tennis Center until she eventually wove her way onto I-95, the one highway that would take her the bulk of the way to the start of her new life.

The highway miles ticked by with uncharacteristic speed, and Jana thought about what this new life might bring. Another new place where she knew no one; an entirely new beginning. Her eyes drifted to the passenger seat of the van, empty with the exception of one item.

"Why the hell did I keep this?" Jana said as she picked up the single white rose. The rose had yellowed and dried over the past few weeks. She held it in front of her. "A calling card. A calling card of a terrorist named Jeffrey Dima. It's time to cut this loose." She lowered the window, then flung the rose out onto the open highway. She left the window open and felt the strong blast of cool air rush into her long hair. She felt new, she felt alive, like she was embarking on the next great adventure.

***

A week later, Jana sat in the waiting area outside a closed office door with her legs crossed.

A receptionist pressed a button on her desk phone, then spoke into her headset. "Yes, sir. I'll send her in." She leaned over her desk and said, "Miss Baker? You can go in there now."

Jana exhaled in one long breath. She stood and straightened her double-breasted jacket, then smoothed her skirt. She pulled her shoulders back and walked toward the office door and placed a hand on the door handle. Her eyes traced the words written on a bronze plaque mounted to the door. It read:

Office of the Director of the FBI
Steven Latent

Don't screw this up, she thought, and pushed the door open.

Brilliant light pouring from the glass wall behind Director Latent silhouetted him where he stood. He walked around his desk and extended a hand.

"Welcome to the bureau, Miss Baker."

Jana placed her hand in his and vice-gripped it. "Thank you, sir. But I don't understand. I haven't interviewed for the position yet."

Latent returned to his leather chair. "Of course you have. You think we normally get the chance to field-test our people before they come to work here? No, we've got all the information we need to make a decision, and I wanted to tell you personally. You put your life on the line for your country, Miss Baker, and your country thanks you for it. Not to mention that I've got Special Agent Chuck Stone's personal recommendation here, and the fact that we've already done your background check."

"I'm very excited, sir."

"You understand you'll start out as a surveillance specialist? You're several years younger than most of our applicants for special agent. You'll have to get some experience and prove yourself if you want to advance to that role."

"Yes, sir." Jana was so nervous she couldn't think of anything else to say.

"Miss Baker, are you familiar with the saying, *some people have a job, others have a career?*"

"Yes, sir."

"Well, what you're stepping into is neither a job nor a career. What we have is a *lifestyle*. Understand the difference?"

Jana thought about the statement for a moment. "I think I do, sir." She nodded her head. "I'm ready, sir. I won't let you down."

"You'd better not. Oh, but there is one matter I'm afraid we have to discuss." His forehead furled. "It's a matter of utmost importance; something that must be handled before we can extend you a formal offer."

"And what's that, sir?"

"I understand you asked Uncle Bill if he would lend you his wife's minivan for the move down here? Ah, he's going to want that back first."

An excerpt from the sequel, The Fourteenth Protocol

Get a free ebook copy of *The Fourteenth Protocol*, book 2 in *The Special Agent Jana Baker Spy-Thriller Series*, today by visiting NathanAGoodman.com/fourteen

Next, read an excerpt:

The Fourteenth Protocol

Over 640 reviews:

Six years have passed since *Protocol One* and Jana has just graduated from the FBI Academy at Quantico, Virginia . . .

A terrorist on the loose, a country in panic, and time is running out.

After an eleventh terrorist attack, the American people are at a breaking point. But when a fledgling special agent stumbles across the one clue that could break the case wide open, she uncovers a secret CIA spy operation and becomes the only

asset that can stop it.

Come inside this spider's web of espionage, conspiracy and intrigue, and witness young Agent Baker's struggles against evil and her own fears as they take her to the edge of the abyss; and the clock is ticking.

An excerpt from *The Fourteenth Protocol*:

Thirty minutes later, the couple left the club and walked down Peachtree. If ever Cade felt like he was being watched, now was that time. Six sets of FBI snipers were deployed on rooftops, each sniper with a complimenting spotter, an agent trained to assist with visualization of targets and communications with other agents. Binoculars focused down from different angles. Lots of encrypted radio chatter was ongoing as groups of agents communicated back and forth. But to Cade and Jana, there was only the whooshing sound of a passing bus, a car horn in the distance, and the dull hum of music permeating from nightclubs in the neighboring blocks.

There were four additional hostage rescue teams deployed at three hundred and sixty degrees around the building. Each team pointed a laser mic at various floors, listening for anything unusual. The agents of the Hostage Rescue Team were keyed up. In their vernacular, they were cocked, locked, and ready to rock. These guys lived for this stuff. To an HRT member, this is what it was all about; this is where they earn their pay. For some HRT agents, this was their first live deployment, although every one of them came out of a military background and had extensive experience in live firefights in the Gulf War.

Jana continued to hold Cade's hand and led him down the wide stairwell off Peachtree Street to the MARTA tunnel below. The tunnel crossed underneath the road to the train platform on the other side. It was somewhat deserted at this time of night, with the exception of a few people waiting on trains, and one Agent Kyle MacKerron, seated on a marble bench at the far end adjacent to the north-bound train line. Kyle wore an Atlanta Braves ball cap and carried a messenger bag over his shoulder. Inside that bag, there was certainly no laptop computer or notepad. Instead, Kyle's MP5 subcompact machine gun lay quiet, hoping beyond hope not to be needed. Cade, one of his best friends, was walking into harm's way, along with a fellow agent. The tough part was Kyle couldn't do anything about it. It wasn't like they could avoid this situation. No, the danger was there, and it was something that had to be done. Cade and Jana would have to face it alone.

Kyle watched them from the corner of his eye as he listened to his earpiece, awaiting the go-code from HRT that Cade and Jana were cleared to enter the building. Once they entered, the twenty-five-minute countdown would begin, and there would be no turning back. HRT watched for the building's guards to change shifts.

Since Kyle was from Savannah and sported a southern drawl, the HRT operators honed in on him like a bug to a windshield; to them he seemed to be tough as nails, and they liked him from their first meeting. To lighten the tension of such an intense operation, HRT loved to invent amusing radio codenames for each other. Kyle would be identified as *Savannah* across any radio chatter. And it seemed only fitting to use call sign *Paula Deen*, in reference to the famous Savannah chef, to identify Agent in Charge Murphy. Although he too was tough as nails, he had a well-known passion for cooking—something his men kidded him about. He across the street on the twelfth floor of the Atlanta Financial Center and would be personally overseeing all ground operations.

Then came a crackle in the encrypted radio signal as Kyle's earpiece barked to life. "Savannah, cheese grits are ready for the oven," chirped the radio. "Savannah, cheese grits are ready for the oven." It was Kyle's signal to give the green light to Cade and Agent Baker to make their entrance.

Jana and Cade busied themselves looking at the rail line map. Kyle removed his baseball cap and ran his fingers through his hair—their signal to enter the building. Without glancing in their direction, he tapped his watch, a reminder that the twenty-five-minute countdown had started. Should they fail to exit the building in twenty-five minutes, the Hostage Rescue Team would breach the structure with what they called *extreme prejudice*. The pair turned and walked through the double sliding doors. To Kyle, the two looked perfectly natural and relaxed, but his insides were eating him alive.

High atop the Atlanta Financial Center, an HRT sniper and his spotter focused. One watched through polished Steiner optics, the other through the Leupold scope of the sniper rifle chambered in .270 Weatherby Magnum.

Cade and Jana disappeared from sight and moved farther down the long, underground hallway, which led from the station platform to the Thoughtstorm building. Since both buildings literally straddled the train line, these entrances became a mainstay for employees to commute to work using the MARTA rail. The HRT team thought it advisable for Cade and Jana to use this entrance so as to avoid the main entrance off of Peachtree Street. Entering down here, they'd be able to access the elevator up to the seventeenth floor without having to walk past building security.

The white hallway stood in stark contrast from the dingy train platform. Its fluorescent lights glowed brilliantly through the translucent laminate material clinging to the ceiling and walls. Cade had never used the tunnel at night, and he squinted against the light. He felt so exposed, like he was walking into the mouth of an alligator. Tiny hairs on the back of his neck stood tall.

Kyle keyed the tiny transmitter in his left hand and whispered into the mic. "Paula Deen, this is Savannah. The cheese grits are in the oven. Paula D, the cheese grits are in the oven."

Cade swiped his keycard across the security bar, and they entered the elevator. It was the same elevator he had stepped into so many times before, but this time it felt like stepping into a honed glass coffin. His stomach had that feeling of having just dropped down the screaming hill of a roller coaster; only this time, the feeling wouldn't go away.

There was no turning back. He turned to look at Jana then began to reach for the button labeled 17 when her hand interrupted his. She darted her eyes upwards towards the small security camera peering at them from the corner. Knowing they may be watched, she wanted to make this look real. The appearance of being young and in love would work in their favor if they were caught, and it wouldn't hurt if they seemed a bit drunk either. She feigned losing her balance to carry off the appearance of being a bit tipsy. But if she told herself the truth, the lines between working this undercover role versus falling for Cade were blurring. She leveled sultry eyes, put her hand on his chin, and kissed him. After a moment, she pressed the button herself,

128

but since it was a secure floor, the elevator door didn't move. Cade swiped his keycard, tapped his security code into the digital keypad, and the elevator was cleared. They were headed into uncertainty.

Jana kissed him again as they embraced for the camera. For Cade, the problem was deeper. He was falling hard; he couldn't help it. And riding up this elevator-to-terror at the same time he was kissing the most beautiful girl in the world represented a paradox he couldn't quite comprehend. He was dizzy. The elevator ride seemed to go on and on in an endless rise. Cade was falling in love with this girl whether she was acting for the cameras or not. When this whole damnable terrorism case was over, he was going to crash, and crash hard.

The elevator rose and a faint chime announced each floor.

Ground, One, Two, Three, Four . . .

Kyle assured him the building guards would be changing shifts right at this moment. If the timing was perfect, they would get to seventeen without being seen. Cade's chest heaved, a sure sign of nerves that had been fraying for days.

Outside, HRT operators pressed headsets tightly against their ears. There were no fewer than twelve pairs of eyes. Each agent pair had a laser mic mounted on a heavy tripod pointed at the Thoughtstorm building. They listened with intent for any sounds inside the building that could signal trouble.

Agent in Charge Murphy, the senior-most agent on the Hostage Rescue Team, broke into the silent radio.

"All eyes, all eyes, this is Paula Deen. You are code yellow. I repeat, you are code yellow. Do not fire unless fired upon. Do not fire unless fired upon, over."

Each operator in the HRT team knew what that meant. Unless

the yellow code status elevated, permission was required in order to discharge their weapons. One thing working in their favor was that the mirrored glass of the building was now completely translucent. The darkness outside the building and the brightness inside caused a reversal of the mirrored shine. They may not have direct communication with Agent Baker and Cade Williams, but on the first sixteen floors, they were able to see inside several interior spaces.

An HRT pair stationed across from the southwest corner of the building had their laser microphone pointed at the uppermost floor. The building's blueprints had revealed that to be the location of the elevator winch, and thus, the most likely place to detect elevator movement. The agent's eyes were closed as he focused on the diminutive sounds emanating from his headset. He heard the distinctive sound of an elevator winch kick into motion and keyed his headset.

"Paula D, this is nine. Paula D, this is nine. The grits are rising in the oven. We confirm vertical movement. I say again, the grits are rising, over."

Inside the elevator, the security camera mounted in a corner near the ceiling leered at them. Jana was unsure if the elevators were also bugged for sound, and she too felt very exposed.

Five, Six, Seven . . . chimed the elevator.

She whispered in Cade's ear.

"Relax, Cade. Whatever happens, it'll be fine." She smiled at him. "Remember, we've got heavy backup outside. There are more guns trained on this place than protecting the White House."

Eight, Nine, Ten . . . the elevator rose.

Cade drew in a deep breath, closed his eyes, and held it.

Eleven, Twelve, Thirteen . . .

His ears began to pop against the elevation. He exhaled hard, blowing out as many jitters as he could.

Fourteen, Fifteen, Sixteen . . .

Jana squeezed his hand.

Seventeen. Cade stopped breathing.

Kyle crushed his hand against his radio earpiece. HRT operator nine said in a whisper, "Paula D, this is nine. The hash browns are scattered, smothered, and covered. Repeat, the hash browns are scattered, smothered, and covered." Kyle shook his head. *Jesus, these HRT guys must all be from the south. Only a southerner would be familiar enough with the Waffle House diner and it's various ways to serve hash browned potatoes to understand the humor.* He smiled and began to appreciate the need to relieve a little tension.

The elevator doors slid open into a vacuum of bleak silence. At the far end of the sterile hallway, the guard desk stood vacant as an empty chair swiveled, letting out a slight squeaking sound. The shift change was happening; the guard had just stepped out.

Cade whispered, "I'm not sure having more guns pointed at this place than protecting the White House makes me feel any better right now." To Cade, the tension was as thick as trying to breathe through a mouth full of peanut butter. They walked across the white tiled floor as the heels of their shoes echoed onto their own straining eardrums. Cade swiped his keycard against the thick metal security door leading onto the server floor. A digital beep was chased by the sound of the door's steel throw-bolt sliding clear. Cade pushed his way through the door and was suddenly terrified that he would see William Macy standing with folded arms on the other side.

Silence. Cade's eyes darted from left to right praying no one would be there. The server floor was empty except for the hum of spinning hard drives and glowing light. Cade had never seen it so quiet. He felt very vulnerable as the pair walked in, Jana

131

pulling him along.

"Jesus, it's freezing in here," she whispered.

"Yeah, they keep it at fifty-nine degrees to keep the servers happy. Most days I don't bother putting my lunch in the fridge."

They walked over to Cade's desk. "Well, this is me. But over there is where we need to go. That's Johnston's office. Pray to God he left his laptop in there. Otherwise, we're hosed."

"Remind me to get you a picture frame or something for your desk. Man, you guys have no sense of decoration," Jana said, still clinging his arm.

Across the radio outside, "All eyes, all eyes. This is Paula D. Any audible signs from the oven? Repeat, any audible signs from the oven? Over."

There was no reply. The skin coating the exterior of the seventeenth floor not only blocked laser mics but also reduced visibility to near zero. It was like looking into the translucent smoke of a forest fire and trying to see what was behind it. As far as knowing what was going on inside the building, HRT was dead in the water.

In the command center, Agent Murphy leaned over. "Christ, this blindness is like waiting for Apollo 11 to clear the far side of the damned moon."

Cade and Jana approached Rupert Johnston's office. Cade sighed in relief, halfway expecting the man to be sitting right there with a "what in the Sam Hill are you doin'" look on his face. The office was empty. On the dark mahogany desk, underneath a stack of loose papers, the black laptop sat sleeping, its lid closed. Cade darted behind the desk, opened the laptop, and held down the power button.

"That smell," said Jana. "It's . . . it's . . . bourbon or something. Damn, where's that coming from?" Glancing in the oblong trash can under the desk, Jana had her answer. She reached in and pulled out the empty bottle of Jim Beam. The lid was on, but a drop of the Kentucky whiskey made an escape attempt down the side of the bottle.

"That's weird," Cade said. "I've never seen Johnston drink. Then again, I've never seen him out of the office either."

"Cade, the smell is strong in here. I don't see any spills anywhere. It's like the smell is fresh."

"Well, let's just get this over with," Cade said.

Just as little LED lights blinked to life on the laptop, the login screen appeared. Jana pulled out a lipstick, pulled off the top, and removed the gel copy of Johnston's fingerprint. She slipped it on her index finger and swiped it over the laptop's scanner. A message appeared on the monitor indicating the print had been authenticated. But then another login screen appeared—this one required a password.

"Shit," Cade said. "Fingerprint *and* password authentication."

"What do we do now?"

"I can get through it, but it'll take a minute."

Cade inserted a thumb drive. Jana focused on the monitor, but became distracted by the array of loose papers fanned across the desk.

"Man, look at all this stuff," she said. "It's all handwritten. Who handwrites anything anymore?"

"Jana, even south Georgia boys know how to write. Check out his diplomas on the wall."

Running her hands through the papers, she said, "And look how old some of this is. These on the bottom of the stack look like they're fifty years old. They're all yellowed." Jana fingered her way through the stack, up to the top. "And these on the top are much more recent. They're all dated. It starts back in . . . 1965."

Without glancing over, Cade said, "Ah, kind of busy over here trying to steal the secret files, remember?"

"There's different handwriting on some of the older ones," she said. "Wow, looks like these were love letters from his service in Vietnam. He must have had a girl back home. I feel like I'm invading something private here."

"What? Private? Oh, yeah, I think he started out as a private during the war."

"Oh, you aren't listening to me." Jana read on. Private or not, she was captivated. It was like peering into a little piece of history you weren't supposed to see. Some of the passages revealed two young kids in love, separated by a god-awful war. A smile spread across her mouth, but as she flipped farther in the stack, her smile disappeared.

"Cade?"

"Yeah?"

"Look at these. Some of them have perfect watermarks on them. Someone's tears fell on these letters. This one is still damp."

Cade looked up, but only for a moment. "Well, they couldn't be Johnston's tears, I can tell you that. I don't think he has tears. And if he did, he'd probably kick his own ass just for crying."

The screen on the laptop went blue, and a message read "Boot from external drive?" Cade clicked *yes*.

"What's it doing?" said Jana.

"We don't have Johnston's password, so I loaded an NT boot registry app onto the thumb drive. The laptop is booting from there."

Jana shook her head at the technobabble. The farther she thumbed forward through the papers, the more recent the dates on the papers became. Jana skimmed faster and faster through the stack and started to realize this was more than a collection of

134

love letters.

"Cade, it's like the rest of this is a journal or something. This part starts about a year ago . . . it's like he's recording all his work."

"His work? What work?"

"His work here. Here at Thoughtstorm," she said. "Holy shit, he's documenting his work here. My God, look at this! Dates and times of e-mail campaigns, names of recipient lists . . . this part talks about some kind of . . . encryption . . . wait, look at this! CIA! Oh my God. He's recording conversations he had with the CIA. Jesus Christ, Cade, this is evidence. This is like, this is like . . . finding the damned Rosetta stone. This is the key to everything we need to tie this all together."

For once, Cade looked up at the papers. His mind was trying to concentrate on two things at once, and it wasn't working.

Jana dug her fingernails into his arm, "Where's the copy machine? I've got to copy this right now."

"Ouch. My, we are old-school, aren't we? There is no copy machine. Server dudes don't copy anything. Here, take out your phone. Use the camera and take pictures of all this stuff. I've got to crack into this damn laptop. Those papers might be the Rosetta stone, but it won't help us much without the actual data."

"Kyle has our phones." Jana's eyes ran across the page at the very top of the stack, the most recent writings. She turned her back to the desk and leaned against it.

"This, this . . . was written today," she said. "He's talking about . . . about . . . it's like he's conflicted. He's talking about blowing the lid on the whole thing, the whole cover-up. But wait . . . look at that. He sounds desperate to blow the whole thing wide open, but he knows he can't. It doesn't say why."

She lowered the stack and said, "He knows he can't? What does he know that we don't know? What's the laptop doing now? You said something about we didn't have his password. That thumb drive thing, it's going to crack his password?"

"No, not exactly. It's going to bypass his password and allow me to set a new one. In the morning, when Johnston logs in, he'll be asked to reset his password. We have to reset our passwords monthly anyway. There's a chance he won't suspect a thing."

Just then, a towering, hoarse voice exploded from the doorway. "Won't suspect a thing!"

Jana and Cade froze in terror, wide-eyed at the oversized man blocking their only exit. It was Rupert Johnston.

"What in the Sam Hill are you doin' at my computer, Williams?! And who in the hell is this?!"

Thoughts raced through Jana's head. Should I draw my weapon? Should we just take the laptop and run for it? Then, a horrifying thought popped into her head from all those months of training at Quantico. Her instructors practically beat it into her head. "If you ever use your weapon, one shot, one kill." The voices echoed like the beating of a drum.

"Uh, ah, um . . . yeah, ah, Mr. Johnston . . .," babbled Cade, "no, ah, well, see we were just in here and . . ."

Johnston was furious, yet his eyes were swollen and brimming with tears.

He yelled, "I said, what in the Sam Hill are you doin' on my computer!"

Then his eyes locked on the papers Jana was holding. "Them's, them's personal!" He lunged forward; his left hand grabbed her neck and wedged her against the wall. The papers splayed out onto the floor.

"Mr. Johnston! No!" Cade yelled, jumping up, his hands on Johnston's crushing, steely forearm.

But as quickly as the rage started, it stopped. Johnston released his grip on Jana's neck and looked at his left hand as though it were a beast beyond his control. Jana coughed violently.

He reeked of bourbon. "I, I . . . I don't even know who I is anymore," Johnston said still gazing at his hand. He stumbled backwards and fell into a heap on the ground, his salt and pepper hair jarring in the process.

Jana's initial shock faded as she regained her composure and cleared her throat. Without anyone noticing, she slipped her firearm back into its holster. She had nearly pulled the trigger at point-blank range. She shook herself off and stood tall. It was like looking at a cross between a petite young woman and someone who'd just faced down insensate evil. The terrified young girl crumpled into ashes and the agent emerged. Jana had crossed over.

"They got their claws into me. I can't even r'cognize muh-self anymore," Johnston said, still staring off into oblivion.

Cade was petrified.

"Rupert?" The softness in her voice was like a fork cutting into Boston Crème Pie. She knelt down and put her hand on his shoulder. "Rupert," she whispered, "it's over now. It's all over. You don't have to be a part of this anymore."

As though he didn't even hear her, he said, "She thought I was dead, ya see."

Jana and Cade looked at each other, bewildered. Johnston seemed to be in his own world where alcohol wedged itself between past and present.

"Darlene . . . Darlene was, Darlene was a waitin' on me."

Jana placed a finger against her pursed lips, signaling Cade to stay quiet. She circled around Johnston's side, knelt down, and glided her hands across his broad shoulders.

Rupert's glazed eyes registered her presence but looked more like he was watching a movie.

"She's a waitin'. You'll see. She's just 'roun' the bend up here. When this here bus stops, you'll see. She'll be a standin' right there at the station."

Leaning behind him, Cade half-mouthed, "What the hell is he talking about?" but Jana held up her hand.

"Tell me about Darlene, Rupert," Jana said.

"See, there was a mistake, see," his speech slurred. "I had done lost a set of dog tags durin' a firefight, and see, sumhow somebuddy foun' them dog tags and thought I was dead, an', an', an', they sent a chaplain to tell Darlene, an', an', an' she thought I was dead. Truth be tolt, I thot I was dead a time er two muhself. And whut, with Jimmy Joe dyin' right in front a me and that, that dollar bill a his." He was still in his own world but focused on Jana now. "Jimmy Joe had this dollar bill in his pockit," his inflection flared, "and when that grenade went off, well, Jimmy Joe was . . . was . . . all a mess." Rupert burst into tears and leaned into Jana's shoulder.

Words choked out of him. "He was all blowed up. He was all over me. And that dollar bill a his . . . it . . . it was stuck to my leg. Just stuck there like sumbuddy done painted it on me. It's stuck on me, an' I kent git it off."

Rupert began clawing at his left thigh at a dollar bill that existed only in his mind.

"It won't come offn' me! I kin never git it offn' me! Help me git it off!"

Jana reached out to steady his hand, but it was futile against his drunken strength.

Jana said, "Rupert! Rupert. Now you stop that. You just stop that." Her voice was strong and firm.

He looked up at her again as a slight glaze of terror melted from his eyes. Jana nodded to Cade and pointed to the laptop; she had Johnston distracted, and the twenty-five-minute timer was running.

"You remind me of my Darlene," Johnston said, the stony façade flaking away. "She was purty. I got a pitcher of us when I was jus' shippin' out. We was standin' there at the bus stop when I was leaving. She looked jes like you." Rupert's eyes wandered far away, and he said, "That picture I got. It's like, like you kin just see it. In our eyes, ya see. Like we was the only two people in the whole world. Two people who got the resta their lives in front of 'em." Heavy tears rolled off his face and landed on his lap.

Cade was making progress on the laptop. He looked at Jana and mouthed "almost there."

Jana looked back at Rupert and saw the shell of a man who looked like he had lost himself down a dark rabbit hole and found his way back up, but when he got there, the world had changed.

"Rupert, it's all over now," she said. "It's all going to be okay. Everything that's been going on here. You don't have to do it anymore. It's over now." She was stabbing in the dark, unsure of his reaction.

Tightened muscular ropes that streaked across Rupert's fore-head loosened.

Jana continued, "I want you to come out with us now. It's time to walk away from all of this. It's time to tell the truth and just walk away." She stole a secretive glance at her watch.

Johnston leaned in toward Jana's ear. His whispering voice was almost childlike. "The doll'r bill, is it gone now?"

The dollar bill symbolized terror experienced in Vietnam. But now, it symbolized the terror of a CIA investigation that had gone wrong.

"It's gone now," she said. "And if you come out with us now, it will be gone forever."

The room went deathly quiet. Jana glanced at Cade, who flashed thumbs-up, nodded his head, then said, "It's done, I've got everything we need."

Jana said, "Rupert, I want you to stand up now. You come with us now."

A breeze of calm soberness drifted across Johnston as the tension in his shoulders eased.

"It ain't that simple no more. Nothin's that simple no more." He looked into Jana's eyes as if talking straight to her soul. "There ain't no way outta here for me. You don' understan'. If'n they find out, God knows what'll happen. I can't git out."

"Rupert, we can protect you. You'll be safe. Come out with us."

"It ain' my safety I'm talkin' 'bout. You don' understand. If I stop—if they find out I'm tryin' to git out—they'll do somepin." He looked far off. "Somepin terrible. No, no. I can't go nowhere . . . I'm all used up."

Jana sat up in fear of the words coming out of Johnston's mouth and what they might mean. She was afraid to ask, but had to.

"Rupert? What do you mean *something terrible?*"

Rupert gazed at his own reflection in the darkened window. "I've never been so ashamed in all my life. It jes, it, it jes got away from me. I thought we was doin' something good. But it jes . . . got away from me. And by then, it wus too late. Too late. I didn't know they was gonna do all that . . ."

"What is it they're going to do, Rupert?" But he wasn't really hearing her.

Johnston looked at Jana. "It's all in them papers, Darlene. Go on, you go on, Darlene. Y'all git outta here and take them papers with ya."

Cade was up and looked at his watch, then mouthed, "It's time to go."

Jana pleaded, "Rupert, please. Please come with us. Do as Darlene says and come with me now."

Rupert watched tears drop onto his trousers. "Yer wrong, little lady. Dead wrong," he said. "It ain't gone. It ain't never gonna be gone. That doll'r bill, it's still stuck right there where it's always been. I kin only think of one way it's ever gonna be gone."

Cade entered the early stages of panic and moved behind Rupert, grabbing Jana by the arm. He pulled her up and noticed the pursing and quivering of her lips, her eyes tight and fighting back tears of their own. He looked at his watch again. Cade knew it was too late for Rupert; the two of them had to go—and go right now.

Jana yanked against him as he tugged her out of the office. "No, wait. Look at his eyes," she whispered. "This is really wrong. He's going to do something crazy."

Rupert stood up and a mechanical blankness washed his face. It was as if all the emotion in the world had drained away. He bent down and reached underneath the desk. A tearing sound was audible as Rupert yanked open a Velcro strap, releasing a hidden handgun from its holster. Cade pulled against Jana. "Oh shit!"

But Jana yanked back again, ripping her arm free. "No, dammit. He's not going to hurt us, he's going to hurt himself!" She screamed, "Rupert! No!"

But Rupert pushed past them like a robot, never feeling their weight. The large .45 caliber handgun pointed forward as he stormed past and headed for the door to the security desk . . .

You've just read an excerpt from *The Fourteenth Protocol.*

Get a free ebook copy of *The Fourteenth Protocol,* book 2 in *The Special Agent Jana Baker Spy-Thriller Series,* today by visiting NathanAGoodman.com/fourteen

Some readers prefer to purchase the three-book series bundle: books2read.com/u/4Dvjd3

To stay informed of new releases by Author Nathan Goodman, visit NathanAGoodman.com/email

Made in the USA
Lexington, KY
19 June 2017